IRRESISTIBLE TEMPTATION

Carnivale Chronicles

ELLE WRIGHT

Elle Wright

Irresistible Temptation
CARNIVALE CHRONICLES

Elle Wright

Irresistible Temptation
Copyright @ 2020 by Elle Wright
Paperback ISBN: 978-0-9994213-4-5

Excerpt from *Her Little Secret*
copyright @ 2020 by Elle Wright
Excerpt from *The Closing Bid*
copyright @ 2019 by Elle Wright

Elle Wrights Books, LLC
Ypsilanti, Michigan
www.ElleWright.com
Editor:
Nicole Falls
Cover Design:
Anita Davis

 Created with Vellum

Emerie Cole is at a crossroads. After a humiliating break-up with her trifling boyfriend, Emerie is forced to find a new home. In the interim, she decides to go to her brother's place to figure out her next step. Only she's not alone. One minute, she is trying to forget about the years she'd wasted with one man. The next, she's kissing the man who starred in too many teenage dreams to count—her brother's best friend.

Celebrity DJ Vaughn Carr made beating the odds a full-time job. From an early age, he learned to open closed doors and step in like he owned the room. Yet, there's one door that should remain closed, one person that should be off-limits—his best friend's sister, Emerie. Circumstances force them in close proximity and, soon, he can't get her out of his head... or bed. The more time they spend together, the more he realizes that he needs her in his life.

The only problem? Convincing her that this off-limits, forbidden relationship can be more than hidden affection and secret liaisons. This can be forever.

For my Granny! Thanks for loving me and making the best oatmeal I've ever tasted. Miss you so much.

Acknowledgments

Oh my word! My 17th book!

God is so good! I'm forever thankful to Him, first and foremost.

To my husband and children, thanks for understanding, for encouraging me to write even when I'm tired. I love you so much.

To my sista friends, love you! You know who you are!

A special shout-out to the amazing readers , bloggers, and awesome writers that I've met on this journey. There would be no "Elle Wright" without your love and encouragement, your enthusiasm and understanding.

Dear Reader

It has been so rewarding to be a part of another amazing anthology. I'm so grateful to the co-founders of Book Euphoria for constantly setting the bar high and pushing limits.

Writing Vaughn and Emerie's story was challenging for me. In the end, though, I'm glad I had the opportunity to do it. It was cool bringing new characters into my world. I don't think I'll let them go just yet. Stay tuned.

Be sure to pick up the other books in the Carnivale Chronicles series. The amazing authors writing these stories are changing the game. I'm honored to be included.

I hope you enjoy the ride!

Love,
Elle
www.ellewright.com

Chapter 1

"*H*ey! I recognize that dick."

Emerie Cole stared at the cell phone that had been passed around to every woman in the salon. The giddy laughter in the room suddenly stopped. Several pairs of eyes landed on her; a gamut of emotions displayed in each of them. *Shock. Amusement. Concern. Pity.* The pity stares were the worst, though.

Her stylist, Kerry, snatched the phone from her and looked at the screen. "Stop playin', girl."

"I'm not playing," Emerie replied in a dull, flat tone. Because that's exactly how she felt in that moment. Dull and flat. And murderous.

Every other Saturday, Emerie, sat in the Hair Sensations salon, cackling with the ladies who shared stories of their dating escapades. It had become a ritual for them to pass around pics sent to them by strangers over the internet. But Emerie had never participated. Because she wasn't single, because she lived with her boyfriend of six years, and because she was committed to her relationship. *To him.*

Apparently, he wasn't committed to her on the same level. Instead of looking for a job, he was sending out dick pics.

"Sis, I'm sure it's not what you think," Kerry whispered in her ear. "It could be anyone's dick. If you've seen one, you've seen them all."

Except that wasn't true. She'd seen many, but there was only one that had a distinguishing birthmark on the shaft, right below the tip. She knew that because she lived with that dick every day of the last several years. The profile name was also a dead giveaway. *MOB Man*. He didn't even have the decency to hide his activity behind an unknown nickname. No, he'd used his initials and nickname for the profile.

"Rie, listen to me," Kerry said. "You can't…"

Emerie was sure Kerry was still talking, but she couldn't hear her any more than she *wanted* to hear her. Her thoughts were running a mile a minute, combing through the past few months, looking for any obvious signs she'd missed or any whispered conversations she'd tuned out.

Maybe it wouldn't have been so bad had she not been supporting them since he'd been laid off from his manufacturing job last year? Maybe she wouldn't be considering catching a case if she hadn't worked like a dog, picking up overtime and working more events than usual? Nah, she would have been pissed either way. Because this was some straight bullshit.

Emerie shook her head; freeing it of those thoughts. No time for regrets or even a sad, sorry meltdown. Definitely no tears. Not even a slight tickle in her throat. But the more she'd tried to hype herself to handle her breakup business, the more she wanted to cry. The thought of all that time wasted working on a relationship that seemed doomed to fail almost from the beginning made her want to throw up. She'd changed parts of herself to "compromise" with him. And the kicker? She'd turned down a dream job for him, for their love. The same love he'd stomped into the ground a little bit more with every month… every day they were together. But this? The. Final. Straw.

"Rie?" Kerry stepped in front of her and jostled her with her knee.

Emerie blinked, focusing on her friend. They'd met in this very chair four years ago when she'd happened to walk into the salon for a cut and curl. Ironically, she'd just broken up with her last boyfriend and needed a change in her hairstyle then.

"Huh?" Emerie swallowed.

"Did you hear what I said?"

"I have to go." Emerie jumped out of the chair, yanked off the cape, and picked up her purse. "I'll CashApp you."

"Wait!" Kerry called after her. "Rie, your hair is still wet."

But Emerie didn't care. She just needed to get out of that damn place and away from the curious stares. Ignoring the calls, she dashed out of the salon and ran to her car.

It only took fifteen minutes to make the drive home. Along the way, she'd tried to think logically. What if there was someone else in the world that had the same birthmark? But even as she tried to make excuses, she couldn't make the pieces fit into a nice puzzle that would exonerate him. Deep down, she knew it was the truth.

When she pulled into the driveway, she took a centering breath before she hopped out of the car. The house was quiet when she entered, no signs of her boyfriend. Which was odd since he was *always* home. The man barely went out to the store or to the gym or to put in a job application.

Walking through the house, she checked the family room, the kitchen, then went into the basement—his man cave. He spent a disproportionate amount of time hidden away in this space. Emerie glanced back at the staircase, checking to see if he'd snuck up behind her.

Eyeing his computer, she approached it and sat down on the chair. By nature, she wasn't an irrational or insecure woman. In all the years she'd been dating, she'd never asked her man for his phone, she'd never followed him hoping to catch him in a lie, and she'd always maintained that if she ever had to do those things, the relationship wouldn't be worth keeping.

Still, she had to know for sure. She clicked on the mouse. The lock screen came up, and she tapped a finger on the desk, trying to figure out what he'd used for a password.

After two tries, she grunted a curse. Finally, she took a chance and typed in his daughter's nickname and birth date. *It worked*. The internet browser was open—to the very website the ladies were looking at in the salon. *Fuckin' asshole*. She scrolled through the many messages in his inbox. Apparently, he spent a lot of time doing shitty things on dating apps.

Her vision clouded as she stared at the screen. The number of women he'd been conversing with—exchanging numbers and meeting at coffee shops and hotels—was straight disrespectful. Now, she understood why they hadn't fucked in six freakin' months. He'd been giving it to random women he'd met in chat rooms. All the while, claiming to love only her. And she'd been a damn fool for far too long.

Standing on shaky legs, she took a few calming breaths,

said a prayer or two. Nothing helped. Livid didn't do what she felt justice. It just didn't seem to be enough of an adjective. Like, seriously… she wanted to hurt him. Which was why she made the decision to leave before he got home. Despite her earlier assertion, she wasn't trying to go to jail for hurting that nigga.

She grabbed the large suitcase she kept in the basement and dragged it upstairs, straight to their bedroom. She picked it up and set it on the bed. Opening one of her drawers, she grabbed the contents and tossed it in the suitcase. She emptied the others just as fast.

Stepping into the closet, she brought out several outfits on hangers and dropped them on the bed. She did all of this on the verge of tears. Thankfully, not one fell. Not even when she heard the side door open, and not when felt him behind her watching her.

"What's going on, babe?" he asked.

Emerie didn't turn to him, because the thin string she was dangling on was liable to snap.

"Babe." She heard his footsteps inching closer but didn't stop packing. He reached out, but she dodged him, brushing past him toward the dresser. "Rie."

She cringed at his use of her nickname. Only people who loved her could use that name. Now, she didn't count him among that group of people.

His hand on her arm stopped her. "Babe, what are you doing? Where are you going?"

"Away from here," she grumbled, yanking her arm from his grasp. She hurried to the bathroom and cleaned out her bathroom drawers. And for the first time, she got a full unabashed view of how she looked. She'd left the salon in such a hurry; her hair was a mess—one side straight and the other side wild and tangled. *Great.*

Emerie let out a shaky breath and one tear streaked

down her cheek. One. Fucking. Tear. Because she'd let that asshole ruin her "me day". Getting her hair done was one of the only things she did for herself on a consistent basis. She loved sitting in Kerry's chair, she enjoyed being pampered. And he'd sullied her salon experience with his community ass dick.

Steeling herself, she cleared out her shower cubby and re-entered the bedroom. He was still there, still looking like he cared.

She stopped, irritated that he was blocking her suitcase. Raking a gaze over him, she scowled in disgust. The black suit he wore fit his six-foot-one, two-hundred-pound frame perfectly. The wine-colored shirt underneath the jacket complemented his brown skin. It was her favorite color on him. Gone was the shaggy, unkempt atrocity that had been covering his face for the past three months, and it its place was a trimmed beard and goatee. Any other day, seeing him dressed like that—looking so fine, so clean, and so sexy—would have made her want to do naughty things to him. But not to-damn-day.

He stepped forward. "Rie, talk to me."

"What?" she hissed. "Get out of my way, Marcus."

"What's going on?" he asked. "Your hair—"

"Shut up, Marcus!" she shouted, slicing her free hand in the air. "Don't say shit to me. With your trifling ass."

Marcus frowned. "What the hell is going on?"

Emerie snorted. "Fuckin' asshole." The need to throw something at him reared its ugly head. She scanned the room, but of course, there was nothing around but little shit that wouldn't matter and the stuff in her hand. Still, she threw her bottle of shampoo toward him. It narrowly missed him. But she sent the conditioner, feminine wash, and loofah at him. And it was the loofah that landed, hitting him on the side of his face.

"Emerie," he yelled. "Stop!"

"You have made a fool of me," she growled, picking up a pillow and swinging it at him.

"What are you talking about, babe?"

Furious that he'd continued this deer-in-headlights act, she jabbed her finger in his face. "You're sending pics of your little dick to random women?"

The absolute truth of the matter was his dick wasn't that small, but once upon a time he'd confessed that *he* thought it didn't measure up. So, she knew it was a soft spot for him.

"I saw your profile on some raunchy dating app, Marcus. At the salon!"

"Look, Emerie."

"I don't want to hear it. Since you're obviously on the hunt for new pussy, I'll just get out of your way." She walked to the other side of the bed and pulled her suitcase to her. Closing it, she zipped it up and set it on the floor.

He stepped closer "Emerie."

She held up a hand, signaling he'd better not come any closer. "Don't," she warned.

"Listen, baby." Marcus scrubbed a hand over his face and the pained expression on his face nearly made her want to comfort him. But she stood still, rooted to her spot. "I don't know what those females told you at the salon. And I don't care. They don't know me. You do."

He's good. And if she hadn't seen the proof for herself, she might have believed him. "Obviously, I don't know you."

He reached out. She stepped back. Marcus didn't let that stop him, though. Cradling her face, he bent to kiss her cheek. She dodged the contact.

"Don't touch me," she said, smacking his hand away.

"Baby, please." He pulled her closer. "Believe me."

Shoving him away, she said, "That's the problem. I don't."

"No." He shook his head. "You can't do this to us. I'm not accepting this."

Frowning, she said, "I don't care what you accept. But what you won't do is get another chance to play me the way you've done." She swallowed. "I trusted you. I worked my butt off for us. While you stayed home and pretended to look for a job, while you took my kindness for weakness."

"Babe, I just had a job interview. I think I got it."

"Good, because you'll need to pay your own damn rent. I'm out."

She brushed past him and hurried toward the front door. She'd come back for the rest of her things later. Right now, she needed to leave.

Marcus followed her. "What, then? You're mad. What you gone do?"

"It's simple. I'm leaving."

"Where are you going?" he asked.

"Somewhere. Else."

Marcus hesitated. "This is some bullshit, Emerie. I told you about those bitches in that damn salon. Kerry is the worst one. She's always trying to down me to you."

"Just stop, Marcus. I saw the profile on your computer. I saw the messages, the promises of dates and sex. No need to keep lying. I already know you're guilty."

"Really, Emerie?" Marcus approached her and tried to take the suitcase from her. She pulled it back. "You're going through my things now?"

She grabbed her coat. He gripped the sleeve and they played a stupid game of tug-of-war until she let go. "You know what? Keep it. I can buy another coat. I can do better than I've ever done here."

"Oh, okay." He narrowed his eyes at her. "You're going to buy new equipment, too?"

She sighed. Emerie supplemented her income with her passion. Music. She worked as a DJ in her spare time. Her CD decks, her turntables, her mixers, her controller… there was no way she'd be able to take everything with her. Her heart hurt at the prospect of losing the investment she'd made into her second career. *I should have thought this through.* "I'll be back for the rest of my stuff later."

"Good luck with that," he sneered. "Since I have to pay the rent now, maybe I'll sell your precious equipment on eBay or something. I'm sure I'll get a nice price for that state-of-the art sound system you purchased last year."

She stepped forward. "Marcus, you better not."

He shrugged, stepping back with an evil smirk on his lips. "Don't tell me what I better not do. This is my house."

Emerie's body tensed and her stomach roiled. A mixture of dread and disgust warred with blinding rage for dominance within her. "Your house, huh. All I know is," she took a deep breath, "my shit better be here when I come back. If not, I will *own* this house. Believe that."

With flared nostrils, he advanced toward her. "Don't threaten me, Rie. Your father won't get anywhere near this house."

Emerie's father was partner at one of the top law firms in Ann Arbor. And he'd been waiting for her to leave Marcus' ass for years. Up until now, she'd kept her relationship between her and Marcus, but she wouldn't hesitate to go to her father if she had to.

"Keep telling yourself that," she grumbled. "Don't try me."

"Ah, I see now." He backed up. "You go through my shit; you walk out on—"

"What the fuck is your problem?" she yelled. "You did this! You cheated on me. Multiple times."

"Maybe you're the problem?"

Emerie rocked back on her heels. "Are you blaming me for your wayward dick?"

"You don't fuck, you don't suck… it's your fault I had to find someone else."

Fury clouded her vision. "Fuck you, Marcus. I had to work. Somebody had to pay the damn bills." Before she could think better of it, she picked up the potted plant near the door, not even caring that the dirt was wet and splashed on her. She flung it at him. He ducked, but it hit the wall and shattered into heavy pieces. Wiping her face, she fought back tears when she noticed the mud on her palm. All of her fight evaporated. Not only did her hair look crazy, but she'd more than likely smeared wet dirt all over her face. *I need to get out of here.* "Go to hell." Swinging the door open, she walked out.

Once she made it to her car, she stuffed her suitcase into the backseat and jumped in. Peeling out, she dialed her sister.

"Hey, Rie Rie," Dana answered. "All done at the salon? Want to have lunch?"

"I left Marcus," Emerie said.

Silence.

"He cheated on me," she told her older sister. "I found out at the salon."

"Rie, I'm so sorry. Come over. We'll talk about it."

"I can't, Dana. The kids are there and I don't want them to see me like this."

Dana was mother to two very impressionable ten-year old little girls, who thought Emerie walked on water. It was not a good look to go there looking a hot ass mess.

"The girls will be just fine," Dana said. "I'm worried about you. Besides, where are you going to go?"

"Lennox is out of town. I can go to his place."

Emerie was the youngest of three. Her big brother Lennox was away on business, and she had a key to his condo. He wouldn't mind if she went there.

"Are you sure? I don't think you should be alone, hun."

"I'm good." *I'm not.* "I just need to get a shower and try to figure out a plan to get my shit from the house."

"I can call Dad," Dana offered.

"No, not yet."

"Okay, call me when you get there."

"Fine." She ended the call and turned up her music, intent on drowning out her loud thoughts. Only it didn't work. Everything that had ever been wrong with her relationship came flooding to mind on the twenty-minute drive from Ypsilanti to Ann Arbor. By the time she'd made it to Lennox' house, she was a wreck.

She parked in the driveway, grabbed her suitcase and prayed she remembered to pack the essentials. If not, she was in trouble.

Emerie unlocked the door and lugged her stuff inside. The house was clean and quiet. She padded to the kitchen and peered at her reflection in the stainless steel. Just like she'd thought... *hot mess.*

Grabbing a bottle of water from the fridge, she opened the cap and gulped it down. She pulled her shirt off and shook her head at the glob of dirt on the front. *My favorite shirt.* Irritated, she took her sweatpants off as well and went into the laundry room. After she put her clothes in the washing machine, she went to her suitcase and opened it. *Thank God.*

Emerie let out a sigh of relief that she'd packed her underwear and bras. But cursed when she remembered throwing her soap at Marcus. Oh well. She'd have to smell like Lennox until she could get to the store.

Snatching her phone from the counter, she headed toward the second bedroom and right into a wall.

"Oh my God!" She blinked. The hard wall had hands that wrapped around her waist to steady her. *And* the wall had a naked chest. "Oh no! Oh shit." She squeezed her eyes closed and raised a hand to cover them for good measure because she was not willing to see her brother without clothes. "I'm so sorry, Len. I thought you were out of town. I didn't mean to just drop by but I had a crazy day. I should have called first," she babbled on.

She stumbled back and bumped into something sharp. *Ouch.* She felt behind her and realized she'd run into the edge of a table or dresser. She scooted to the side and tripped over something else, nearly taking an "L". *Shit.* Once again, the hands gripped her arm to hold her upright. Jerking out of the hold, she actually did fall this time, right on her tailbone.

She cursed. "I thought you were out of town," she repeated, eyes still closed for dear life. "I... Oh God."

"It's okay. You're fine."

Emerie's eyes popped open and she dropped her hand. Mortified, her mouth fell open. Because the man staring at her with a devilish grin on his perfect lips was not her brother. It was her brother's best friend and her childhood crush. *Vaughn Carr.*

Chapter 2

$\mathcal{V}$aughn Carr had seen the world a few times over. As a celebrity DJ, he'd played clubs and music festivals in the United States and abroad. He'd toured with popular artists, produced hit songs, and drank beer with some of the most important people in the music industry. Women followed him from venue to venue, just to get him to take them home or wherever—which he'd happily done on more than one occasion. And men wanted to hang out with him because he brought the women. Vaughn had basically seen it all. Well, he *thought* he'd seen everything he could ever want to see. Until now.

Now, Vaughn found himself staring at the one woman he shouldn't be ogling, with her brown skin, those shapely hips, and pouty mouth. *Damn, she is lovely.* Even with a streak of mud across her cheek and her half-done hair, she was beautiful in an innocent, off-limits, touch-her-and-get-your-ass-beat type of way. It was wrong to be even the slightest bit amused by the way she tried to scramble to her feet, covering her breasts with one arm and her other hand trying to hide her…

Clearing his throat, he reached out a hand.

She smacked it away. "Don't," she warned.

"Let me help you," he said. "I promise I won't touch anything else but your hand."

Emerie eyed him warily, before she placed her hand in his and let him pull her to her feet. But he tugged her too hard and her soft body crashed against his, setting off feelings that he shouldn't be having. It was inappropriate to imagine anything other than smores and kumbaya when it came to Emerie. He shouldn't be thinking about hot wax and doggy style.

"Thanks," she mumbled, putting some distance between them. She muttered a string of cute, Emerie-style curses.

Vaughn recognized the exact moment she remembered the state of her undress because her eyes widened and her hands were back in place, trying to cover the areas he was pretty sure were seared on his brain. He had a very active imagination.

"Gosh, don't look at me," she hissed. "Turn around."

"Rie, come on." He did as she asked. "We grew up together, like siblings."

That part was true. Vaughn had known Emerie for years and they were *supposed* to be like brother and sister. It was also false, because there was nothing brotherly about the way he'd looked at her. Or the way his body reacted to the sight of hers. But he thought it might help her feel better.

She snorted. "Thanks."

It sounded like sarcasm, but he couldn't be sure. "I swear I didn't see anything." *Much.* He heard shuffling and more cursing behind him.

"Okay, you can turn around," she said.

Slowly, he turned. She stood in front of him, the heavy

comforter from the bed wrapped around her and that flush still on her face. "Hey, Rie."

With one hand on her hip and the other clinging to the comforter for dear life, she asked, "What are you doing here?"

"Hey, Rie," he repeated.

"Hi." She let out a heavy sigh. "Please answer the question."

Vaughn couldn't hide his smile if he wanted to. And he didn't. "I'm here for Rhonda's scholarship ball next Saturday."

"Oh, okay." She nodded rapidly, without meeting his gaze. "I plan on being there."

That didn't surprise him. Emerie and Rhonda were close, despite their age difference. "Good."

"That still doesn't explain why you're *here*." She pointed down at the floor. "In this house."

"I talked to Len and he mentioned he'd be out of town." He raked his gaze over her petite frame, starting at her crazy hairstyle and dropping to her eyes, her nose, then lingering on her mouth. She looked like a little fairy, graceful and magical, beautiful and delicate. "I have several meetings next week in the area. I was going to book an Airbnb, but he offered his place."

When Vaughn traveled, he often sought out rentals so that he could have privacy and space to practice or mix his music before whatever event he was doing.

"Great," she muttered, hugging herself.

"So why are *you* here?" he asked.

Emerie bit down on her bottom lip, but she continued to stare at something behind him or the wall or the floor. "I'm currently without a place of residence."

The last time he was in town, she was living with her

boyfriend. Frowning, he asked, "Don't you live with Marlon?"

"Marcus," she corrected. "And no." She pointed her toes into the carpet. "Not anymore," she added under her breath.

"Is this a recent development?"

"Yeah, today."

Interesting. "I'm sorry."

She nodded. "I guess I'll be hearing a lot of that in the coming days." Emerie glanced up at the ceiling.

"What happened?" he asked.

She let out a weird whimper-like grunt. "Nothing. So, um, can you please put on some clothes?"

Vaughn blinked. "Oh shit." In his effort to make her feel like she shouldn't be embarrassed that he'd seen her in her panties and bra, he'd completely forgotten that he was basically naked. "I'm going to…" He pointed toward the hallway. "I'm getting dressed."

"Please do that." She saluted, before averting her gaze again.

Without turning around, he backed out of the room. Vaughn rushed to the bathroom. *Shit.* He'd left his suitcase in the second bedroom, where Emerie was still wrapped in a comforter.

Slowly, he walked back and peeked into the room. Emerie paced the room, talking to herself and flailing her hands wildly. She'd always been composed, rarely letting anyone see her sweat. She was also kind and giving, funny and intelligent. Now, he could add sexy as hell to that list. He should technically scratch that particular adjective because, *again*, she was off limits.

He cleared his throat, hiding his smile when she froze and turned her back to him again.

"I really hope you're dressed," she murmured.

Stepping further into the room, he said, "My bags are in here." Emerie sucked in a sharp breath when he reached in front of her to grab his suitcase. "Sorry," he grumbled.

"It's okay."

He glanced at her, noted the slight tremble in her chin and prayed she didn't cry. Tears and Emerie didn't mix and would only serve to make him want to hurt whoever made her cry—just like he'd done years ago.

The little boy who'd stolen her popsicle one summer day had never even looked her way again after Vaughn was done with him. The jerk who'd kissed her behind the bleachers during their middle school dance never tried it again once he and Len had a little talk with him. And during his senior year of high school, he'd beat some sophomore's ass because the fool dared to spread a false rumor about her. Vaughn considered it his duty to protect his best friend's little sister at all times. That compulsion hadn't changed over the years because he wanted to throttle that punk ass Marcus.

"Rie," he murmured.

She dropped her head. "Please, Vaughn." Her voice was a shaky whisper, a plea.

Vaughn didn't want to push her, but he also didn't want to leave her alone like this. More importantly, he didn't want her to *feel* alone. He reached out to touch her shoulder but thought better of it and pulled his hand back.

"I'm going to go to my sister's house," he announced. "I can just stay there."

A tear streaked down her cheek, and she wiped it away. She still didn't meet his gaze, though. And he wanted her to look at him. "Okay," she said. "Tell Rhon I said hi."

He hesitated. In the end, he decided to honor her wishes. "I will."

"Thanks."

With a heavy sigh, he walked out of the room.

"Vaughn!" Rhonda pulled him into an embrace. "I'm so happy you're here."

He held on to his sister for a moment. "It's good to see you, sis."

She pulled back, cradled his face. "You look good, brother."

He smiled. "So do you. For an old lady."

Rhonda smacked his shoulder. "Oh, shut up." She grabbed his hand. "Come in here."

Soon as Vaughn entered the house, he heard screams as his nephew zoomed toward him. He lifted his three-year-old nephew in his arms. "What's up, Eli?" He held up a hand and his nephew gave him a high five.

"Hi Unco," Eli said.

"What you been up to, lil man?"

"I can count!"

As Eli start to recite his numbers at a higher-than-normal decibel, Vaughn walked through the house to the family room. Rhonda picked up his little niece and brought her to him.

"See your uncle," Rhonda said, in a sing-song voice. "He's here to see you."

The last time he'd seen his niece, she couldn't even open her eyes for long, let alone hold her head up. Now, she was alert and watching everything.

"Switch?" Rhonda asked.

He handed Eli to Rhonda and took Luna from her mother. "Hey, little cutie," he said. He kissed his niece's brow. "She's getting so big."

Luna giggled and grabbed his lips.

"I know. I want time to stop," Rhonda danced with Eli —who'd continued to count to ten over and over again. "Are you hungry?"

Vaughn shrugged. "I can eat."

He followed Rhonda to the kitchen and took a seat at the breakfast bar. She put Eli in his little chair. "I made chili."

"Sounds good."

Rhonda set a bowl of chili in front of him and took the baby. "Eat."

Vaughn picked up his spoon and dug in. A few minutes later, Rhonda joined him.

"So what's been up?" she asked. "You've been traveling all over the place. It's great to have you home."

Smiling, he nodded. "It's good to be here."

Rhonda was more than his sister. She'd been a stand-in mother to him. At seventeen, his father kicked him out of the house because he'd dared to question the restrictive rules imposed on them. His big sister hadn't hesitated. She took him in, even though she had a little baby of her own. They'd helped each other. Rhonda supported him through his last year of high school and he babysat his niece while she worked fifty-hour weeks at the local auto manufacturing plant *and* took classes at the community college.

"Where's Elena?" he asked. Usually, his oldest niece would be front-and-center, telling him about school and tennis and social media.

"She's out with her friends. They went to the movies."

"Hope she's out with *girl* friends," he grumbled.

Rhonda waved a hand at him. "Please, you know I don't play that dating at thirteen."

"Good. I don't want to have to threaten a little boy."

She giggled. "You've always been a little too overprotective."

Vaughn thought about Emerie, wondered if she was okay. "I have to. Where's Elijah?"

"At work," she replied. "Like always. I told him no patients at the scholarship ball."

Rhonda had married Dr. Elijah Walters five years ago. The pediatrician worked a lot, but he treated his sister well. Which was all that mattered to Vaughn. She'd been through a lot in her life. During her second year of college, she'd gotten pregnant with Elena. His hardcore religious parents turned their backs on her. Without their financial support, she'd been forced to drop out and get a job. Rhonda worked her way through college and dental school, through sheer will and tenacity. And now she'd started a foundation for young single mothers, with a focus on education and career planning.

"I'm sure he'll be there." He squeezed her hand. "I'm so proud of you, Rhon."

She shot him a watery smile. "Thanks. I just want to offer support to young mothers who may not have a village to help them. I wish I'd had that from our parents."

"They will. Because of you."

Rhonda pointed at him. "Don't make me cry."

He laughed. "No crying allowed."

It was something they'd always told each other—when they struggled with life, when they were upset about their parents, when he moved out of the state.

"Where are you staying?" she asked.

He rubbed his face. "I was staying at Len's."

She shot him a questioning glance. "Was?"

"Emerie is there," he told her. "She broke up with her boyfriend."

"Oh no!" Rhon shook her head. "That's crazy. I just saw them a few weeks ago. We all went bowling."

Vaughn envisioned Emerie at the bowling alley. *Did she bowl with that same hop before she let the ball go?* He shook his mind free from that thought. Because he shouldn't be thinking about her at all. "Sounds like a bad time," he muttered.

"Just because you spend your days surrounded by scantily-clad women at clubs doesn't mean the rest of us don't enjoy wholesome fun."

"Hey, I'm wholesome. And did you just say scantily?"

She giggled. "Oh, shut up."

"Listen, I—"

The baby let out a wail, and Rhonda hopped up to get her. Then, Eli screamed. For the next five minutes, he rocked his niece, while Rhonda tended to his nephew. His intent was to ask if he could take the spare room for the night until he could find new accommodations.

He lifted up his niece, in an attempt to stop the whining. She giggled as he did a silly beatbox. "See, you're okay," he told the baby, bouncing her up and down.

"Vaughn, you might not want to do that." Rhonda carried Eli over to them. "She still spits up often."

He grinned at his niece. "She's fine. And she's not crying, so—"

The first projectile spit-up hit him in the eye. "Shit," he whispered.

"Sheait," Eli mocked.

"I mean, damn," he corrected. "Shoot." The next batch of puke landed on his top lip. The horrid smell made him gag. He held the tiny offender at arm's length. The little terror had the nerve to laugh harder, then proceeded to throw up yet again. This time it landed on his shirt.

Instead of helping him, his sister cracked up. "I told

you. You never did listen." She snatched the baby from him and tossed a container of baby wipes to him. "I can throw that shirt in the washer for you. That soy formula is hard to get out."

And the strong smell pretty much ensures this shirt will end up in the trash. "It's fine."

"I'm so sorry." But the smirk on her lips indicated she was anything but sorry. "I can grab you one of Elijah's t-shirts."

He pulled out several wipes and scrubbed the shirt. "No, I'm good. Just…" He held his breath as he scooped off a splatter of throw-up from his sleeve. "This smell could kill someone."

"It's not that bad." She cooed at the baby in her arms, the spit-up master. "You're just not used to it."

I don't want to be used to it. In fact, he was sure this might be effective birth control for the foreseeable future. "Whatever. Listen, I need to ask you something."

"Mommie!" Eli ran into the kitchen, bare bottomed, with his pull-up in his hands. "I boo boo."

His eyes widened as his nephew held up the pull-up.

"Baby, that's great!" Rhonda's eyes lit up, then dulled when she peeked into the pull-up. "Oh no. What did I tell you about going boo boo in the toilet? Not in the pull-up."

Eli did a little dance, obviously not understanding the importance of using the bathroom *in* the bathroom. "I need a new pull-up." Without another word, he dropped the used pull-up onto Vaughn's foot and ran out of the kitchen.

His gaze dropped down to his sullied sock. Vaughn loved his sister and his nieces and nephew. But it had been many years since he'd changed diapers or bottle-fed an infant. Quiet space and boundaries had ruled his life in recent years. Which was why he preferred to rent homes instead of hotel rooms. It allowed him to practice before a gig and close out the world when he needed peace and quiet. Staying with his sister—no matter how much he missed her—was not an option. *I'm out of here.*

A couple of hours later, he left his sister's house with promises to drop by tomorrow to see Elena and Elijah. His best bet? A hotel. Just for the night. Yet, he found himself driving back to Len's house, to temptation that he didn't know existed until he'd seen Emerie earlier that day, clad in her underwear and looking like a perfect angel.

When he pulled up to the house, he sighed. *It's Emerie. I can do this.* After all, they'd seen each other at their best and worst. They'd been in each other's lives for years and nothing had ever happened between them. Nothing *would* happen between them. Because she was little Emerie. He remembered her at eight, with her braids and light-up gym shoes. He remembered her at eleven, with her bracelets and books. He knew her at thirteen, with her braces and lip gloss.

Emerie's big, beautiful doe eyes didn't matter. Her sexy voice and firm breasts didn't matter. Her full lips didn't matter. That ass, though… he couldn't convince himself it didn't matter. Because since he'd caught a glimpse of it, the image had been seared into his brain. Emerie mattered, too. Which was why it was so important that he kept his wayward thoughts in check—*and my dick, too.*

Vaughn walked up to the door and knocked. Using the spare key Len had given him wouldn't be wise. A moment later, Emerie opened the door.

"Vaughn?" Her gaze dropped to the suitcase in his hand. "You're back?"

"Yeah." That one word was all he could manage because something changed between the last time he'd seen her and now, something had happened between his little pep talk in the car and now. For the first time, he saw Emerie for the woman she was today—beautiful, smart, capable. She'd showered and pulled her hair back into a ponytail. She wore a pair of oversized sweats and a plain white tank. And she'd been crying. He could tell by her red eyes and the pieces of tissue stuck to her cheek. "It's late."

She stepped aside, letting him know it was okay to come in.

He brushed past her, trying to ignore the citrus scent in her hair. "I just need a night. I'll find another place tomorrow." Vaughn rolled his suitcase over to the wall and turned to face her. "I'll take the couch."

Emerie scrunched her nose. "What's that smell?"

Vaughn pointed to the stain on his shirt. "That smell is reason-number-one why I couldn't stay with Rhonda." Then he pointed to his foot. "And the second reason is why I don't have on a sock right now."

She giggled, and it was like fresh air to congested lungs. "Wow, you should probably burn that shirt. And I don't even want to know what happened with the sock."

He chuckled. "No, you don't. Let's just say potty training was a bust."

"Yikes." She smiled. "I made some food. Are you hungry?"

Vaughn had already eaten, but he wanted what she had on the stove. "I could eat."

She motioned toward the hallway with her forefinger. "After you take a shower."

Later, they sat on the couch eating chicken stir fry. Emerie watched TV, while he watched her. She hadn't said much, other than polite talk. But it wasn't uncomfortable.

"Are you going to tell me what happened?" he asked.

"Nope," she chirped.

Chuckling, he said, "Tell me how you really feel."

She set her fork on her plate. "It's not you, Vaughn. I just don't want to talk about it. I need time to think."

"About what you're going to do next?"

Nodding, she picked at the edge of the blanket on her lap. "It's not exactly an ideal situation."

"Losing the relationship?"

"Actually, the relationship probably needed to end. Losing time, the house, my dignity… that hurts."

Vaughn fought hard to keep his thoughts to himself. He sensed she just needed his ear. "I bet it does."

"I can't even…" She sighed heavily. "I don't know what to do."

He reached out, moved a strand of hair from her forehead. It wasn't an awkward move, or even something he'd never done before. But this time, it felt like more than a simple touch. It was a connection, one that had shifted from the innocent interactions they'd had in the past.

"You'll do what you have to do," he told her.

She peered up at him, searched his eyes. "You seem very confident."

He shrugged. "Because I am. The Emerie I know wouldn't let this stop her."

"How do you know that? It's been a long time since you've seen me."

"Not that long," he said. "What? A year?"

"Two years."

He stared at her. It *had* been two years since he'd seen her. "I remember."

She averted her gaze. "Me, too."

The memory flooded through his mind. They were in New York. She was there with her girlfriends and he was working. In hindsight, that might have been the moment he started to see her differently. Because he remembered everything about that interaction—what she wore to the club, how her hair was styled, who she'd danced with. He also remembered keeping an eye on her, watching her on the dancefloor in her skin-tight leather pants. Even then, he'd told himself he was making sure she was good. He'd told himself that he needed to look out for her in the sea of strangers vying for her attention.

After he was done with his set, he'd gone to her and invited her for coffee. They'd spent the rest of the night catching up, talking until the sun rose. Then, he'd dropped her off. They hadn't even touched that night, but it felt like they had, like they'd morphed into alternate versions of themselves for a few hours.

"It was a good night," he said. "And since we did talk for a long time that night, I know that you're still that same girl—woman—who bugged me until I showed her how to work a controller, how to turn a record."

"You hated when I followed you around with my old turntable."

"I did," he admitted. "You were the original playa hater."

Her head fell back as she laughed. "Oh my God, I remember that night. You thought you were so hot, bringing that girl back to our house."

"And you strolled into the basement with that damn turntable and a Run DMC album."

"In my defense, I was laser focused on learning everything I could from you."

"And you did."

Vaughn had taken Emerie under his wing, taking her to parties, teaching her techniques. He was proud to call her his first student, and he'd followed her DJ career through the years. He knew she'd worked her way through college DJing.

"I guess I did. I'm still not better than you, though."

"Yet," he said, with a shrug.

Emerie leaned into him and he wrapped his arm around her. "Thanks, Vaughn."

He rested his chin on top of her head and tried not to bury his nose in her hair. "You're welcome. You got this."

She wrapped her arms around his waist, hugging him. "I do, don't I?"

He laughed. "Absolutely."

Chapter 3

"*S*hoot." Emerie stood on the tips of her toes and tried to reach the brown sugar on the top shelf of the cabinet. Frustrated that she still couldn't grab it and cursing her brother for being a typical tall person who stored shit where vertically challenged people couldn't reach them, she pulled over a chair and stepped on it.

"What are you doing?"

She yelped and nearly fell off the stool. Gripping the cabinet door, she took in a few deep breaths and threw a small bottle of cinnamon at him. "You scared me, Vaughn!"

He raised his arms up "Sorry. Need any help?"

Emerie finally grabbed the brown sugar and stepped down. "No. And don't walk up on me like that again." She turned off the oatmeal on the stove. "You're up early. How did the couch treat you last night?"

"I've had better couches."

She laughed and finally braved a glance his way. "You're silly."

And still fine as hell. At least he had on clothes today—

dark jeans and a plain white t-shirt that showed the outline of every single muscle in his chest and stomach. The same muscles she'd often imagined tracing with her tongue.

Emerie blinked, willing herself not to go there. She wasn't a little fifteen-year-old girl enamored with her brother's best friend anymore. She was a woman... enamored with her brother's best friend. In her defense, though, she might be a little traumatized from her crazy breakup with Marcus. Maybe she was just feeling a little reckless? Because a few hot ass dreams and many hot day fantasies were all it ever was—never anything more. Except, it felt like more in New York two years ago. And it felt like more last night.

He leaned against the wall and folded his arms over his chest. "What are you making?"

"Oatmeal."

Ah, I remember you love the oats."

She scooped a heaping helping of oatmeal into her bowl, dropped a pat of butter and sprinkled brown sugar inside. "You know why."

"Because it's like eating breakfast with your Granny."

Emerie allowed herself a smile. "You remembered."

Sunday mornings were always for her grandmother. They'd eat oatmeal and watch *Matlock* reruns. It was their thing. When she died a few years ago, Emerie still couldn't let go of the tradition. Despite the pang in her heart when she thought of the heartbreaking loss, she'd chosen to honor Granny by doing what they'd enjoyed best.

"I remember a lot of things," Vaughn said.

Their eyes locked and her stomach clenched. Clearing her throat, she tore her gaze away. "Want a bowl?"

"Sure."

Emerie reached up to grab him a bowl from the cabinet. "Butter or..." Her words died on her tongue when she noticed the heat in his gaze, the way his eyes raked over her. Suddenly, she felt a little self-conscious and strangely powerful.

"You're staring," she croaked.

A slow smile spread over his mouth. "Maybe."

"At what?"

"You."

Emerie sucked in a sharp breath. "Are you staring at my ass?" she joked, trying to lighten the mood from hot and hotter to light and funny.

"Maybe. A lot more to it than when you were thirteen."

She laughed. "Really? So you're flirting with me?"

Vaughn shrugged. "I don't know. Haven't decided yet."

Her mouth fell open.

"You seem shocked," he continued.

She closed her mouth. "I'm not. Men look at my butt all the time."

"What?" He narrowed his eyes at her. "Who does that?"

"I don't know," she teased. "But I'll be sure to ask every guy their name when it happens."

"Ha. Funny."

"Hey, I'm just trying to lighten the… hot."

"Are you hot, Emerie?" The low rasp of his voice hit her right in her core, made her feel all kinds of mushy. *And wet.*

Yes. "No," she lied. "We're friends. Why would you make me hot? It's March in Michigan. Still cold as hell outside. The heat is probably on in here." She fanned herself dramatically. "I'll have to check the thermostat."

"Okay," he said.

She didn't miss the sarcasm in his voice. He didn't

believe her and she couldn't blame him. Emerie had always been a horrible liar.

"I hope I didn't embarrass you," he said.

"Never. Like I said, it happens. By the way, you…um," she scratched her temple, "have a nice chest. I mean, abs. I mean… oh whatever. Butter and brown sugar?"

"White sugar," he said, with a smirk. "Lots of butter."

She nodded. "I seem to recall you liked a little oatmeal with your butter."

He barked out a laugh. "Hey, it's not like it has a taste or anything. Mostly, it's just blah."

"So why do you want some?"

He shrugged. "Because you're eating it."

She snuck a glance at him. *Oh boy.* "Okay."

They didn't bother going to the table. Instead, they stood in the kitchen and enjoyed their bowls of oatmeal in silence.

Emerie finished her meal and rinsed out her bowl. "I know you're here for the ball, but that's a week away. What are your plans while you're here?"

He joined her at the sink. "Meetings. Want to set some things up for the summer."

She took his bowl and washed it out. "Are you thinking of spending time here this summer?"

Emerie didn't know why the thought of him being around for longer than a few days made her feel so good. Or why he smelled like lemons and leaves. Or when she started caring about how he smelled.

"I'm thinking about it." He rested against the counter while she washed the rest of the dishes. "Luna is six months. I haven't seen her since she was a baby. Eli is talking up a storm. Elena is going to movies with her friends, without her mother."

She glanced up at him, observed his profile as he stared ahead. "You miss them."

"I do."

"I know they miss you, too." She wiped the countertop. "They seem to grow like weeds."

"Tell me about it." He rubbed his jaw. "I want them to know me, ya know?"

She nodded. "I know. Dana's kids are getting so big. I spend as much time with them as I can. We have auntie-niece days. Pedicures and movies and laser tag."

"Sounds like a good time."

"Oh, it is. We have a lot of fun shooting people in the dark."

"Every time I come to town I think about going to see my mom. But then I change my mind."

Emerie squeezed his arm. *Oh my, his bicep is like a rock.* "I saw your dad at the store last week."

He dropped his head. "Really?"

"Yeah. He ignored me."

Vaughn snorted. "I'm not surprised."

Emerie hated that Vaughn didn't have a relationship with his parents. As far as she knew, he hadn't spent no more than a few minutes with either of them since they kicked him out of the house years ago. All because he didn't want to be a blind disciple of their church. He'd wanted to create music; he'd wanted to be free.

"Maybe he didn't see me," she offered.

"He probably did. They're getting older, though. They could be sick and I'd never know. I'll never understand how a parent could just cut their kids out of their life, like they meant nothing, like they *are* nothing."

"I'm sorry," she said.

He gave her a sidelong glance. "Me, too." Vaughn

walked to the refrigerator and pulled out a bottle of water. "What are you doing today?"

Emerie was grateful he changed the subject. He'd been there less than twenty-four hours and they'd already shared more than she'd shared with Marcus in months. Even though, they hadn't really talked, which was weird.

"I have a party Friday night. And my equipment is at the house. I'm going to try and get it today."

Vaughn raised a brow. "Try? Why do you have to *try* and get it? Can't you just go over there and pick it up?"

Marcus' words rang in her head. She hoped he wouldn't actually sell her stuff, but she was sure he'd give her a hard time about coming to get it. That wouldn't stop her from going, but she wasn't looking forward to it.

"Well…" She hunched a shoulder. "He did threaten to sell my stuff. So there's that."

"Wait, what?"

"When I broke up with him, he—"

"I'm sorry, but that's some bullshit." Vaughn walked away and came back. "He actually said he would sell your shit?"

"Yes, but it's only been a day, so I doubt that's happened. I wouldn't put it past him to change the locks, though."

Vaughn's jaw clenched. "Oh, you're going to get your shit. Because I'm taking you to get it."

He walked to the door and she followed him. "Vaughn, what are you…? What are you doing?"

"I just told you. We're going to that house and we're getting your equipment. And I want him to say something to me." He placed his hands together, like he was praying. "Please let him say something to me."

"But—"

He gestured to the door. "Let's go."

Vaughn drove them to Marcus' house in his rental SUV. They parked a few houses away.

He glanced over at her. "Ready?"

She nodded rapidly. "Let me do the talking, okay?"

"Maybe." He jumped out of the car.

"Vaughn!" She called, fumbling with her seatbelt frantically. Finally, she was able to free herself and she hurried to him. "Don't do anything crazy."

"I promise I won't do anything crazy. Because my fist against his jaw isn't that crazy. Or even out of the realm of possibility. One thing I can't stand is a bully. And he's threatening your livelihood."

Emerie placed a finger over her lips. "Shh. It's fine. I told you, let me handle it. I know how to handle Marcus."

"Really?"

"Yes. I broke up with him."

He titled his head to the side. "Why?"

"I told you I didn't want to talk about it," she hissed.

She rubbed the back of her neck. They were standing in the middle of the street, probably looking crazy as hell. And he wanted to ask questions about one of the most humiliating things in her life.

Vaughn folded his arms. "Tell me why."

"No."

"Okay, I'll get him to tell me." He stalked off.

His long strides made it difficult to keep up with him. She had to jog ahead to beat him to the door. She turned and blocked him from walking up to the porch. "Vaughn, please. This is my fight."

"Fight, huh? Is he really going to fight you over your stuff?"

"No, that's not what I meant. I'm just…" She shook her hands at him. "If you can't let me handle this, you can go home."

He snorted. "Like hell. I'm not leaving you here with him."

"Then listen to me."

His eyes bored into hers, waiting for her to talk. "Well?"

"It's complicated. But I got this. Let me handle it."

Vaughn let out a heavy sigh. "Fine. You talk. I'll finish if I have to."

Satisfied, she said, "Deal."

Emerie walked around to the side of the house and tried her house key. When the door clicked, she let out a slow breath. Turning to him, she mouthed, "In and out."

Vaughn nodded, his eyes hard, his face tight. "Whatever."

She stepped into the house with Vaughn right on her heels. The house was quiet, much like it was yesterday. *Maybe he's with one of his hoes?* That thought made her angry all over again.

"Most of my equipment is in the office," she whispered, pointing toward the hallway. "Follow me."

Emerie rushed to the office and opened the door, sighing with relief when she saw her stuff was still there. She brushed a hand over the Pioneer DJ DJM-900NXS2 Professional Mixer she'd saved up to purchase. *Thank God.* Behind her, she heard movement and whirled around to find Vaughn unplugging the CD Decks, then the turntables, then the microphone. She joined him, hurriedly gathering her things. Because her work required her to be mobile, she had several rolling carts that made transporting her heavy stuff easier. She also used a duffle bag for her smaller items.

She slipped her laptop into a briefcase. "Oh shit."

Vaughn glanced at her. "What?"

"My personal laptop. It's in the bedroom, under the bed."

"Go get it. I'll finish up here."

Emerie made her way to the bedroom. Her MacBook was right where she had left it. She grabbed both her phone charger and her laptop charger. Scanning the room, she spotted the same bottle of soap she'd thrown at Marcus in the corner. She rushed to get it.

I might as well get everything I can, she thought.

Decision made, she entered the closet and pulled out a weekender bag she kept for overnight trips. She stuffed a few more items from the closet into it. Emerie grabbed shoes, belts, scarves, shirts… everything she could carry. The bag was full quickly, so she carried the rest out of the closet, intent on getting a trash bag for the rest.

"What are you doing?"

She jumped, dropping all of her things on the bed. "Marcus," she breathed. "You're here." She glanced in the hallway. *Where the hell is Vaughn?*

Marcus approached her slowly. "You broke into my house."

"I'll be out of your way in a few minutes. I needed to get my things."

He shook his head. "I don't think so. You're breaking and entering, and I'll just go ahead and call the police."

Emerie let out a frustrated sigh. "Seriously, why are you doing this?"

"Maybe I'm sick of your holier-than-thou attitude. You act like you've never done anything wrong. And the minute I mess up, you're ready to throw me away."

"Oh, please. You threw this shit away with your community dick. Why can't you just be a man and let me go?"

"Emerie, I'm not playing with you. Your ass is going to

jail and *my* equipment will be sold tomorrow. In fact, I already have a buyer."

Her shoulders fell. The last thing she wanted was another repeat of yesterday. She just didn't have it in her to give him all of her energy today. "I'm not going to argue with you again. My equipment is not yours to sell. And if you're as smart as you say you are, you won't press the issue."

Emerie hadn't told her parents anything. She hadn't even told Lennox, even though she'd basically moved into his place. But she would. She just didn't want him to cancel the rest of his trip to rush to her side. Because her big brother would in a heartbeat. And her father would jump at the chance to bring Marcus to court, since he'd never cared for her ex-boyfriend.

"Oh, I'm smart enough to know the law," he sneered. "You moved out and now you're here. You entered my property without permission."

"Move out of my way," she hissed.

Marcus grabbed her arm. "I don't think so."

"Let me—" Something yanked her forward and she nearly slid onto the floor. Bracing herself on the bed, she turned to see Marcus hemmed up against the wall, Vaughn's hand around his throat. *Oh no*.

"Tell me again why I shouldn't beat the shit out of this punk ass muthafucka?" Vaughn growled.

Marcus had the sense to look terrified. Probably because he *was* a punk ass muthafucka. Hell, she'd do Vaughn one better. Her ex was a punk ass bitch.

Emerie approached Vaughn. "Don't kill him," she said, her voice flat. "You can let him go."

"Oh no," Vaughn said. "Me and Marlon have to get something straight."

"It's Marcus," she muttered.

"I don't give a fuck," Vaughn retorted.

"What took you so long?" she asked.

"I figured you'd need trash bags to get all of your clothes and stuff." Vaughn motioned to the floor where he'd dropped a bunch of bags. "Finish packing," he ordered.

"Seriously, Vaughn." She tapped her foot against the floor. "You could kill him. He looks like he can't breathe."

While Vaughn and Marcus had similar height and build, Marcus was no match for Vaughn. He knew it too, which was why she suspected he hadn't uttered a word. *Did Vaughn cut off his circulation for real?* Marcus had never been in a fight in his life. He'd grown up with wealthy parents who'd believed violence was never the answer for anything. Surprising, considering he'd threatened her multiple times since she'd discovered his infidelities.

On the other hand, Vaughn spent his youth scrappin'. He couldn't go a month without fighting someone in high school. It was part of the reason he'd been labeled a "bad boy" by a lot of his peers and teachers. And he was a black belt. So, she was sure that hold was uncomfortable for her ex. Not that she cared about his discomfort. She just didn't want to have to bail Vaughn out of jail for attempted murder.

"Hey," she squeezed Vaughn's arm. "Please?"

Vaughn muttered a curse, then turned his glare on Marcus. "I don't give a fuck whose house this is. If you get that close to her again, if you even look like you might want to touch her, I *will* beat the shit out of you. And nobody will be able to stop me. Now, here's what's going to happen. I'm going to let you go and you're going to let her get her shit and get the hell out of here. Okay?"

Marcus nodded.

"Don't do anything stupid." Vaughn patted his hip with his free hand. "You don't want to try me."

Emerie's eyes widened. "You have a gun?"

"Shut up, Emerie," Vaughn grumbled. "Pack up."

She backed up slowly, keeping her eyes on the situation. "I'm packing."

"No, you're not." Vaughn finally let Marcus go. Her ex-boyfriend coughed violently, his chest heaving. "Where are your speakers?" Vaughn asked, as Marcus continued to gasp for air.

"In the basement," she told him.

"I'm going to bring them up." Vaughn glanced down at Marcus. "Distance. In fact, why don't you get the hell out of here?"

"My house," Marcus said, finally. "You can't kick me out."

"Yes, I can. And I will. I'm giving you a chance to leave on your own."

Marcus glared at her before he walked out of the bedroom.

Vaughn turned to her. "Hurry up."

Emerie grinned as Vaughn left the room. After all these years, he was still her champion, he still took care of her. He'd once promised he would have her back like a big brother should—although nothing about him or their interactions screamed brother. It scared and thrilled her at the same time. She loved the way he made her feel precious and powerful at the same time. *So not good*.

"Thanks for today." Emerie handed Vaughn the last box.

He stacked it in the corner of the spare bedroom at Len's house. They'd just returned from her ex-boyfriend's house, and Vaughn had helped her organize her many boxes and all of her equipment.

"You're welcome," he told her. "If you need to go get something else, let me know. I don't want you going there by yourself."

"Trust me, I don't want to have to go there again."

He must have asked her a million times if she'd grabbed everything. Vaughn didn't trust that fool not to get rid of everything she owned. "I'm just sayin'," he said. "I want you to have everything that means anything to you."

For the first time since they'd left that morning, she smiled. "I do. Thanks to you."

She walked out of the room and he followed. Emerie stopped at the fridge and pulled out two bottles of water. Handing him one, she headed for the couch and plopped down.

"I might have to get my dad involved," she admitted softly. "I was trying to do this without him, but I feel like Marcus will be vindictive."

"That's because he's a sorry ass nigga."

She rested her head against the back of the couch and peered up at the ceiling. "I wish I had planned this better. I was so angry, Vaughn."

He hoped she would finally tell him why she'd broken up with that fool. "Are you ready to tell me what happened?"

Emerie swallowed. "He cheated on me. With multiple women. I found out at the hair salon."

That's why her hair looked like that yesterday. "That's fucked up. Was it with one of the women there?"

"Honestly, I don't know." She turned her head and shot him a sad smile. "I found out because he'd sent a pic of his penis to one of the ladies there. I'm not sure if she'd ever seen it up close and personal. But the fact that he did that really sucked."

"Damn," he muttered. "Did he confess?"

She shook her head. "No. He tried to deny it all the way up until I told him I'd seen the proof on his computer. Then, he turned mean and evil."

Emerie told him about Marcus' job woes, how the idiot sat at home and sulked when he was laid off from his job. She explained how she'd taken on so many side jobs, they'd barely had a chance to see each other. She'd worked her ass off for her ex-boyfriend because she thought that was what people in relationships should do.

Vaughn didn't want to tell her that she was wrong because he didn't think she was. She'd fought for something that was important to her and ended up with egg on her face. For that alone, Vaughn wanted to drive back to that house and kick the shit out of that punk. Then, he wanted to do it again for everything else the man had done to make her cry. Giving in to the impulse to break that man's jaw would have been easy for Vaughn, but she'd asked him not to hurt Marcus. Her voice, her plea saved that guy from an ass-kickin'. Otherwise, it would have been on and poppin', all over ol' boy's precious house.

"I felt the distance between us," she continued. "But I chalked it up to our busy lives."

"It's not your fault, Rie."

She closed her eyes and a tear streaked down her face. "It is. Because I should have paid attention. I shouldn't have ignored the signs, but I was comfortable."

"Still, he's the one who cheated. That's on him."

"Vaughn, you're just saying that because—"

He gripped her chin and turned her face to him. "I'm saying that because it's true. You deserve better than him. You deserve a man who won't lie to you and won't cheat on you with random women on a dating app. Who does that anyway?"

She smiled. "A lot of people."

"A lot of stupid ass people," he said.

Emerie giggled. "You're so funny."

Tracing his thumb over her cheek, he whispered, "You're going to be okay without him. He's going to need you before you ever need him."

"You're just saying that because you're like my big brother."

Vaughn didn't know how to respond to that. Because what he was feeling in that moment was nothing that a big brother should feel for his little sister. What he felt was everything he'd told himself *not* to feel for her.

He'd seen her vulnerability when Marcus tried to attack her, and that made him want to protect her even more. She didn't deserve what she got from the man that was supposed to cherish her. Emerie only deserved love and light, because she'd given those things freely to him and the other people in her life.

Leaning in, he rested his forehead on hers. All words escaped him, because he was so close to her he could smell the mint on her breath, her soft perfume on her skin. The atmosphere around them changed, and he knew if he didn't back away, he'd pull her closer. *Specifically, on my lap.*

"Vaughn," she whispered.

"Yes?" He circled her nose with his, cradled her face in his hands.

"You're kind of flirting with me again."

He smiled. "I'm definitely doing more than flirting right now."

Emerie pulled back, her eyes wide. "Why?"

Once again, the answers evaded him. Simply put, he didn't know. He just knew that he liked it. "What if I said I don't really know why I'm flirting and I kind of don't care? Would that be good enough for you?"

"When you say you don't care, what does that mean?"

"It means that I'm not spending any more time debating with myself on why this isn't good or why it's wrong."

"Don't you think it's kind of soon to have this conversation right now?"

He peered into her eyes. "What do you think?"

Emerie bit down on her bottom lip. "What if I said I don't know what to think and I really *do* care?"

"I'd say tell me more."

Emerie broke away from him then, bolting to her feet and pacing the floor. "Okay, so this is weird, right?" She rested a hand on her hip. "I mean I just broke up with my boyfriend. You helped me move my stuff out of his house. You almost killed him."

He snorted. "I didn't almost kill him."

"You did," she argued.

"Whatever. Let's not talk about that right now."

"Fine. You could have really hurt him—for me. Now, we're sitting here, almost kissing."

"We didn't, though."

"Because I moved. If I had stayed there," she pointed to the couch, "you would have kissed me."

Vaughn chuckled. "Probably."

"See!" She raised her arms out at her sides. "That's weird, right? We've known each for a long time. Why is this happening?"

Vaughn stood and approached her. "I told you I didn't know."

"You also said you didn't care. But, I care."

He frowned. "Why do you care?"

"Because... If you kiss me, things change. I don't know if I'm ready for things to change."

Vaughn had never wanted to kiss a woman so much in his life. He'd never wanted to taste a woman so badly. For a very brief, crazy ass moment, he thought he might die if he never had the chance. But he only wanted to kiss her if she wanted it too. The part of him that knew when a woman was attracted to him felt that she was, but she had to say it before he made the move.

"Rie, if you're not ready, then we don't do it. It's that simple."

Her eyes softened. "Really?"

Vaughn nodded. "Yeah."

"That's good to know."

"You're in charge," he added. "If you want to forget about this, I'll never bring it up again."

He'd stopped short of telling her he'd forget about it because he knew that wasn't possible. And he wouldn't do that, he wouldn't lie to her.

"Thanks," she said. "I appreciate that."

They stood there, staring at each other for a moment. "Vaughn?"

"Yes, Emerie?"

"I don't think I'll forget about it."

A wave of relief washed over him. There was something about unrequited affection or love that had always seemed fucked up to him. He'd vowed to never be the one carrying a torch for someone who didn't want him.

"Good," he said. "I won't either."

"But I don't think I can handle anything more right now."

Right now. The words settled in his gut, sparked a different type of hope. "I understand."

"Thanks." She wrapped her arms around his waist,

hugging him to her. And he let her, reveling in the connection. "Vaughn?"

"Yes?"

"I'm glad you're here."

He rested his chin on the top of her head, and this time, he gave into the urge to bury his nose in her hair. "Me, too."

Chapter 4

"Aw, Rie Rie!" Kerry stepped into the house and pulled Emerie into a strong hug. "I'm so sorry."

Emerie held on to her friend for dear life. She hadn't seen her since the infamous dick pic incident, nearly a week ago. After a moment, she pulled back and smiled.

Kerry wiped her cheeks. "No tears. That's a good thing."

"I've cried them all out."

Laughing, Kerry said, "You mean you're not really a machine."

Emerie let out a humorless chuckle. "Not at all."

Kerry looked around the condo. "This is nice. I keep telling your brother I'm the woman for him." She waggled her eyebrows. "He just likes to pretend I'm not."

Emerie laughed. Her friend had a massive crush on her brother. But Len had never looked at her as more than a friend. Up until a few of days ago, she thought she had a similar vibe with Vaughn, her innocent crush. But he'd gone and changed things between them.

Since that night, the one when he'd defended her from

big, bad Marcus and almost kissed her right there on the couch, they'd avoided the subject. They'd eaten dinners together, watched movies, and played cards. But he never brought it up. He didn't even sit next to her or hug her or look at her the way he usually did. It was almost like he'd turned off Flirt Vaughn and turned on Brother's Best Friend Vaughn. She couldn't say that she liked it. *Actually, I hate it.*

Kerry set her bag on the table. "Is this where you want me to set up?"

Emerie nodded. "It's fine. Thanks for doing this." She pulled her hair out of the ponytail. "I re-washed it this morning."

Kerry waved a dismissive hand at her. "Girl, please. I'm never going to let you go out there looking busted. Unless you run out before I can stop you. And then not answer my calls when I try to come over and fix it."

"That was a bit dramatic," Emerie agreed. "In my defense, I didn't feel like I could stay there with the women who'd seen my boyfriend's dick in living color."

"If anything, you should be honored. It was pretty impressive."

"In theory," she mumbled.

Not that sex was bad with Marcus, though. It just wasn't the best she'd ever had. The extent of their sexual relationship was simple missionary and the occasional doggy style. He never wanted her to be on top because he needed to be in control. Oh, and oral was a bust. The more she thought about things like this, the more she wondered why she wasn't shouting for joy at the end of it.

"Tragic," Kerry said, pulling out the blow dryer, flat irons, and edge control from her bag. She rummaged through the bag for more stuff. "Such a shame."

"Right?"

"What have you been up to? Sit." Emerie did as she was told and Kerry oiled her hair. "You haven't answered any calls."

"I'm sorry, Ker. I just needed time."

"I'm just playin' with you. Not really, but I do understand."

"I've been laying low. I went to get the rest of my things the other day. I'm sure I left something there, and I'm just praying it isn't important to me because I can't count on him to not trash it."

"Seriously? He's such an asshole."

"An asshole that tried to blame you and the ladies at the salon for what he did."

Kerry pointed a rat tail comb at her. "That's bullshit. But I can't say I'm surprised."

Marcus had never liked Kerry. He'd always made it a point to paint her in a negative light. Probably because he knew her friend couldn't stand him and had made it no secret.

"You probably don't see this now, but you're better off." Kerry parted her hair in sections. "He doesn't deserve you. He never did."

Emerie felt a tickle in her nose, the one that signaled she might cry. Again. Her thoughts drifted to her conversation with Vaughn. It had been a long time since she'd let anyone see her cry, but she'd let the tears fall with him. And he'd comforted her, he'd made her feel safe. Then, he'd made her feel other things. *Wanted. Attractive.*

"Okay, that's enough talk about him. I can't…"

Kerry squeezed her shoulder. "Done. No more Marcus talk. Good riddance."

It took ten minutes for Kerry to blow Emerie's hair dry. She immediately started to straighten it. "Want to try something different with your hair? For your gig tonight?"

Emerie had booked a club appearance in Detroit via a referral from a friend at a Detroit radio station. It was at a restaurant-slash-lounge. Friday was their biggest night. Hundreds of people showed up, celebrated birthdays, and danced. It was a huge opportunity to expand her brand and possibly do more appearances at that spot.

"Yeah, let's do something different," Emerie said. "I'm in the mood for curls."

"I'm coming out tonight."

"Yay. I'm so glad you'll be there."

"If you need a host, I'll do it."

Emerie giggled. "The radio station is handling that part."

"Okay, I know we said we wouldn't talk about Marcus, and this isn't really about him, but I hope you know you can stay with me. I have room at my house for you. I mean, I have that big four-bedroom home and it's just me, so…"

"Aw, thanks."

Emerie appreciated her friend's willingness to open up her house to her. She wasn't sure she would take her up on the offer, though. She'd already contacted a realtor and started the search for a new place, and she didn't want to have to move twice. Len would be okay if she stayed there in the interim, even if he didn't know she was there. He'd called her a few times, but she'd avoided talking about Marcus. She'd even convinced Vaughn not to say anything.

"But I'm going to just stay here until I find something." Emerie continued.

"Have you started looking already?"

Emerie told Kerry about her preliminary search. She'd already seen a few condos that she liked in Canton, which was about eighteen miles from Ann Arbor. It wouldn't be a bad commute to work at *Michigan Medicine Health System*.

"I just want to make sure I can get to work easily," Emerie told her friend. "Because you know that traffic getting to the hospital is ridiculous."

"True. What about work? Have you been this week?"

Emerie worked as a cardiac sonographer and she enjoyed what she did. It just didn't make her as happy as being in a sound booth or on a platform playing and creating music for people to enjoy. "I took the week off. My boss was very understanding."

"I hope so. You've been there for a long time."

Emerie sighed. "I'm thinking of taking a leave from work. Just until I can get myself together."

"Really? That's different for you."

"I know, but I feel like it's the best thing for me right now."

Emerie had always been the type to do what was needed. She worked, she came home and took care of her house, and she worked some more. She'd been burning the candle at both ends for so long, she didn't know how to stop. Taking a leave had been a consideration for her for a while, even before she'd ended her relationship with Marcus.

She wasn't hurting for money, but now she needed to purchase a home or condo. It would be nice to not have to dip into her savings for a down payment. So, she wasn't even sure if she *could* take a personal leave from her day job.

"Who knows, maybe you can make it happen." Kerry straightened a piece of her hair. "You definitely need the time—" The sound of a key jiggling in the lock interrupted her friend. A moment later, the door opened and Vaughn stepped in. "—off."

Vaughn grinned. "Hey."

"Hi," Emerie said. It was more like a breathy whisper.

Vaughn in any outfit—or a towel—was fine. But Vaughn in a leather jacket, jeans, and boots was freakin' out-of-this-world hot as hell.

He dropped his keys on the table. "Hey, Kerry."

"Hey," her friend said. Her voice was more like a low rasp. "I didn't know you were here."

Vaughn gave Kerry a hug. "Been here since Saturday."

"Oh," was Kerry's reply.

Emerie didn't dare say anything because she knew what her friend was thinking. They'd talked about Marcus, work, and real estate. But she'd purposefully avoided mentioning Vaughn.

"Alright, heffa," Kerry whispered against her ear. "Soon as I get you alone, I want to know why you've been hiding this from me."

Emerie choked on the water she'd just sipped.

"With his fine ass," Kerry muttered under her breath.

Unable to help herself, Emerie cracked up. "Oh God. You're ridiculous."

"What's been up?" Vaughn grabbed a Pepsi from the fridge. "Still working for someone else when you could be working for yourself?"

"Don't start," Kerry warned.

It was a conversation she'd had with Kerry herself, but her friend had been resistant. Emerie couldn't blame her, though, because her friend had already traveled the entrepreneurship road before. A year ago, Kerry owned one of the best salons in the city of Ypsilanti—with her ex-husband. When the marriage ended, he'd ruined the business. Kerry had to start all over from scratch.

"Why wouldn't you save that booth rent you're paying and re-invest it into your own business?" he asked.

"Because I'm not ready yet," Kerry admitted.

"That's honest." Vaughn leaned against the counter.

"Let me know when you're ready to make that leap, or if you need investors in your product."

Kerry laughed. "If you're really offering, I'll definitely keep that in mind."

They chatted about work and fun for several minutes while Kerry finished Emerie's hair. And Emerie tried hard not to stare too long at Vaughn, or even think about his lips and how they'd feel on hers.

Kerry finished Emerie's hair and patted her shoulder. "You're all set, Rie Rie."

"Thanks." Emerie stood and stretched. When her eyes locked with Vaughn's, she was caught by the heat blazing back her. The way he looked at her... *Oh my*. It felt like she was a small insect caught in a large spider web. She couldn't look away if she wanted to. Luckily for her, she had a best friend that picked up things fairly quickly.

"Rie Rie?" Kerry nudged her, breaking the trance because Emerie had to actually focus on not falling forward on her face.

Tugging her shirt down, Emerie glared at her sneaky friend. "Yes?"

Her friend coughed in an exaggerated, fake way. "My throat is dry. Can you grab me a bottle of water?"

"I'll get it," Vaughn offered.

When he walked to the refrigerator, Kerry elbowed Emerie. "Oh, you need to spill for real."

"Shh." Emerie glanced back at Vaughn, then turned to Kerry. "Be quiet. There's nothing to spill," she whispered.

"What the fuck ever," Kerry grumbled.

Vaughn approached them again and handed Kerry a bottle of water. "I have to make a call," he announced.

Emerie smiled. "Okay."

"Good to see you again, Kerry."

Once Vaughn disappeared around the corner, Kerry

smacked Emerie's shoulder. "Girl, you are straight playin'. What the hell was that?"

"Shut up," Emerie hissed. "He can hear you."

"I don't care." Her friend crossed her arms and narrowed her eyes. "So you have been staying in the same house with that man and just forgot to tell me?"

"I didn't forget. I just didn't think it was relevant."

"Oh!" Her friend raised her hands and pretended to shake her. "It's very relevant."

"How? It's not like we haven't lived most of lives near each other."

"Yeah, as fuckin' kids. He's very adult now, and so are you. And you're single?"

"As of last week?" Emerie tossed her empty bottle into the recycle bin.

"Still, that look he gave you. And the way you responded? That wasn't some innocent best friend's little sister look. That was foreplay."

Emerie swallowed. Hard. "I know what you're think-ing, but I…" She clamped her mouth shut because she couldn't even think of an excuse. Her friend was right. The way he'd looked at her felt more like a caress than a stare. Because every nerve ending she had was buzzing in antici-pation of his touch, of actual skin-to-skin contact. "Fine. It was hot, okay? But do I have to remind you that I'm coming off a long-term relationship. I can't just get with Vaughn Carr."

"Yes, you can." Kerry pointed at her. "Did you see him? Tall, dark, and fuckable?"

Shaking her head, Emerie walked away from her friend. "Shut up."

Kerry followed her. "Seriously, he's just the type of man that can put you on the straight and narrow, veer you right off the Marcus road."

"At what cost? Besides, I'm already off that road. In fact, I'm headed so far in the opposite direction, I don't even want to look back."

"Look back at what?" Vaughn entered the room again.

"Nothing."

"Marcus."

Vaughn smirked at the simultaneous answers from her and Kerry respectively. "Oh, okay. But I hope Kerry was the one telling the truth. Because you do need to leave that asshole behind permanently."

"Right?" Kerry said. "She also needs to—"

"Kerry, it's time for you to go," Emerie interrupted. She packed up her friend's stuff and shoved the bag in Kerry's arms. "I'll see you tonight."

"Alright," Kerry muttered. "I'm gone. But think about what I said."

"No need. Thank you. Bye." She waved at Kerry. "I'll CashApp you."

Slamming the door, she leaned against it, her eyes closed. She counted to ten, taking in even breaths. When she opened her eyes, Vaughn was staring at her again, a soft expression in his brown eyes.

"What?" she asked.

"That was interesting," he replied, with a raised brow. Almost like he knew something she didn't.

"I have to get ready for tonight."

"Oh, yeah. Your gig."

She nodded. "I need to arrive early so I can set up."

"I should come check you out."

"You should. But don't you need security or something?"

He frowned. "No, I think I'm good."

"You're a celebrity. You might need a bodyguard or something."

His gaze dropped to her body, then traveled from her toes up to her face. So slow she thought she might die from the intensity of it. But he didn't do anything, he didn't approach her, he didn't touch her.

"How about I just drive you?" he suggested.

"Oh, my friend is coming to pick me up. He usually takes me to my gigs in Detroit, helps with the equipment."

Vaughn clenched his jaw. "Does he stay for the whole set?"

"Yeah. Hunter's cool. We went to high school together. You'll probably remember him when you see him."

His gaze flicked toward the ceiling before meeting hers again. "Okay, I'll see you there."

The awkward feeling that accompanied his exit made her wonder what she'd done to change the temperature in the room from hot to cold. But she couldn't think about that right now. She had work to do.

Chapter 5

*V*aughn entered the venue late. The place was jam-packed with people in the foyer, in the small waiting area, at the bar, on the dancefloor. It was a typical club atmosphere, women dressed in everything from jeans to booty shorts. In March. As he made his way through the place, he scanned the crowd, checking out who was in the building. It was a habit for him. He needed to see who was there, in case he had to protect himself later.

Right away, several people noticed him and approached him, offering handshakes and wanting to snap selfies. He posed for a few but wasn't really interested in milling around. He'd come for one reason—to see Emerie in action.

The bass was loud, the music was hype, and everyone seemed to enjoy the vibe. He smiled when his eyes landed on the platform, on her. Emerie was standing there, a frown on her face, one hand on the controller and the other on the CD deck. She bobbed to the beat, her shoulders and hips swaying. And she looked like a freakin' goddess up there. Her hair was flowing down her back like waterfalls. She wore leather pants and a low-cut strappy shirt.

Vaughn couldn't help but be proud of her. She'd delivered a flawless mix that pulled people who probably wouldn't have danced otherwise to the floor. Couples twirled around; ladies jumped up to do a line dance.

One of the ladies stopped dancing to slip him her number. He shook his head, not interested in what she had to offer. He approached the platform.

"Vaughn Carr?"

He turned to find some guy in front of him with an outstretched hand. Instead of shaking it, he gave him a head nod. "What's up?"

"I'm Hunter," the guy said. "Emerie's friend?"

"Oh, okay." Vaughn still didn't make a move to shake the little dude's hand.

Why she thought this fool would be protection for her made no sense to him. The man probably couldn't fight his way out of a crowded club to save his life. Safety was important in this business. Some people got crazy, some people thought they could intimidate DJs or maybe even steal valuable equipment. Vaughn needed to have a talk with Emerie about this.

Hunter dropped his hand. "Rie told me you were coming. I just wanted to introduce myself again. Let you know that she's in good hands with me."

Vaughn resisted the urge to laugh. *Good hands with Lil Hunter? Yeah, right.* "Good to know."

"I make sure she's safe."

Nodding, he struggled to find the right words to describe how he felt in that moment. The threat was there, waiting to be said, but he was sure Emerie wouldn't appreciate him telling her friend that if he didn't ensure her safety, he'd have to deal with him.

"The restaurant reserved the booth next to the platform for Emerie's guests," Hunter said. "If you want something to eat, I'll call the waitress over."

"Thanks," Vaughn said. "I'm good for now."

Vaughn glanced up at Emerie again. She was so engrossed in what she was doing she didn't even notice him step up on the platform. He stood beside her for a minute, watching her, studying her movements and her technique. She was in a zone, effortlessly transitioning from one popular beat to another. She'd learned quite a bit since the last time he'd seen her work. Where she used to be a little frenzied, she was now controlled. Where she used to be a little unsure, she was confident.

Up close, she looked even more beautiful, sexier. Even in the dim lighting, her skin glowed like a beacon of light in dense fog. And she smelled like heaven. Vaughn couldn't explain it, he couldn't even reason with himself about it, but he wanted her. In a way that made everything in his life tilt on its head. It didn't make sense because he'd known her since they were kids; he'd seen her happy and sad, calm and angry. Now, he wanted to see her in a different way, without clothes, on top of him, riding him. He wanted to kiss her until she didn't remember anyone before him. *I'm in trouble.*

Finally, she brushed against him and realized she wasn't alone. Her eyes widened when she turned to him. The smile on her face made his stomach clench. "Vaughn!" She hugged him. "You made it!"

"I did."

"Oh shit." She turned and continued her mix. Glancing at him over her shoulder, she said, "Give me a second."

Once she was done, she put on a break playlist.

"What did you think?" she asked.

He grinned. "Amazing. You know how to work the room."

"That's high praise from you. I've watched you long enough."

And I'm seeing you in a way I never thought I would. "I'm glad I could teach you something."

She bit down on her bottom lip. "You did. Man," she clapped her hands together, "this is such a rush. I can't believe this crowd."

"You reeled them in well."

"Want to do fifteen minutes?" she asked.

He shook his head. "This is all you. I'm here to watch." *And pray that I don't do something crazy, like kissing you in front of the entire club.*

"Promise to let me know where I can improve and chime in if you want to show me something I don't know?"

Vaughn smirked as images of him showing her a thing or two—in the nude—played in his mind on an endless loop. "I will."

"Did you meet Hunter?"

"Yeah," he grumbled. "We need to talk about your entourage. You should probably have someone on your team that can actually defend you if something pops off."

"Vaughn, I'm not a celebrity DJ. Who's going to try something?"

"You never know, and I can tell you that if he lets something happen to you, he'll need a hospital after I'm done with him."

Emerie arched a brow. "So violent. Maybe you need to see someone about that."

"I have a better idea."

"What?"

"How about you dismiss your little friend and let me take you home?"

She hesitated. "Is that all you want to do?"

Wait a minute. "Are you flirting with me, Rie?"

Her mouth curved into a smile. "Maybe." She winked. "Maybe not." Emerie turned and segued into another mix.

Hours later, he escorted her to his rental, loaded up her equipment, and set off for Len's house.

"Your friend didn't seem too happy when you told him you were riding home with me," Vaughn said.

"Hunter?" she asked. "He's fine. I'm sure he's probably happy because his girlfriend lives in the city and he can go to her house."

Vaughn officially felt like a jealous idiot. "I didn't know he had a girlfriend."

"Why would you? You were so mean to him back there."

"You noticed, huh?"

Emerie giggled. "It's hard to miss."

The thought of her dating or doing anything with another man didn't sit well with Vaughn. Again, he didn't know why or how this happened. "I'm sorry."

"Don't apologize to me. When I told Hunter you were in town, he was so excited. He said he'd followed your career since high school."

And now Vaughn felt like a jealous asshole. "Wow."

"He's been there for me," she admitted softly. "Someone I could talk to that didn't want to protect me or have sex with me."

Vaughn slid her a guilty glance. He wanted to protect her *and* have sex with her. Did that disqualify him from the role of confidant?

"It's hard to find friends like that," she added. "I appreciate him. He's going to propose in a few months. Been saving up for the ring."

"That's cool."

"Yeah. Really cool."

"Did you talk about marriage with Marcus?"

She snorted. "God, no. We were together a long time, but I wasn't keen on marriage. He brought it up many times, but I always changed the subject."

"Why?"

"I don't know. Just another one of those things that made this break-up the right thing to do. Why continue to waste time with someone I can't envision spending forever with?"

Vaughn thought about what she'd said. "Good point."

He'd never thought about forever with anyone for that very reason. He couldn't see himself with anyone for the rest of his life. Mostly, he'd thought of right now. Which job would pay the bills right now. Which sandwich he wanted to eat right now. Which woman he wanted to take to bed right now.

"Have you ever felt like something bad was actually good?" she asked.

The story of my life. Especially right now. "Actually, yeah."

"I kind of feel like this breakup was my breakthrough. Don't get me wrong, he did hurt me. But it wasn't the worst hurt I could imagine. I feel like I can do anything now. I can move into my own place. I can *afford* my own place. I don't need him. I *never* needed him. For once, I can focus on what *I* want, *where* I want to be, *who* I want to be."

"And you didn't feel like that with him." It wasn't a question. He knew the answer because he'd felt the same way when his father kicked him out all those years ago. Hurt that his parents could discard him so easily, but free.

That one moment changed everything in his life for good. *Something bad, something good*.

"Right." She sighed. "Right."

They rode the rest of the way in silence, but Vaughn's loud thoughts blared in his brain. Back at the club, she'd seemingly opened the door to exploration between them. Now, he couldn't stop thinking about the consequences or the implications of that open door.

He pulled into the driveway and gripped the steering wheel. Vaughn had never been nervous to go inside an empty house with a beautiful woman before. But here he was. Nervous.

"Emerie, I—"

"Vaughn?"

They both laughed.

"Sorry, go ahead," he said.

She shifted in her seat. "I flirted with you at the club."

"No," he said sarcastically.

Emerie smacked his shoulder. "Stop. I'm being serious."

Vaughn grabbed her hand and brought it to his face. With his eyes on hers, he kissed each of her knuckles. Then, he held her palm to his mouth. "Rie," he murmured against her skin.

"Oh," she whispered. "I mean, huh?"

He brushed his lips over her wrist, up her forearm to her bare shoulder, her neck, her jaw, her chin, and finally… her mouth. Cradling her face in his hands, he deepened the kiss, slipping his tongue in her mouth and stroking it against hers. She tasted like mint, chocolate, and freedom. She felt like home.

Eventually, though, he had to break the kiss to breathe. When he did, he rested his forehead on hers. "Damn," he muttered.

"I know," she breathed.

"Rie, I'm not sure this is something we should do. Or even if it's the right time."

"I know," she repeated.

"But I want to."

"I know." She squeezed her eyes shut. "I mean, me, too."

"I need to know you're sure about this. Because we're going to cross a line here."

She giggled. "We're destroying the line."

Vaughn leaned in and brushed his mouth over hers. He traced her bottom lip with his tongue. "If you don't know, or if you're not sure, I'm going to have to go to my sister's house tonight."

Emerie kissed him. Hard. "Come inside, Vaughn." Then, she got out of the car and walked to the front door.

Vaughn sat still in the car, debating with himself on whether he could actually do this. Sleeping with her, making love to her would be a game changer. But when she turned to him and smiled, he knew he had no choice but to follow her.

Chapter 6

*E*merie had barely opened the door before Vaughn pulled her into his arms and crashed his lips to hers. He kissed her deeply and passionately, like he couldn't get enough of her. Her body was on fire, burning in places that had been cold for years.

Vaughn kicked the door closed and grumbled, "Bedroom."

"Lock the door." She took off and ran to the bedroom, but he caught her right before she crossed the threshold and scooped her up in his arms. Seconds later, her back hit the mattress and he was kissing his way... *Oh shit.* He was kissing his way up her body. *Where are my pants?* Because she certainly didn't remember him pulling them off.

His lips, though. Those talented lips branded her, made her want to push herself into him. She'd never felt so wound up, yet so free in her life. He hadn't even touched her core with his fingers—or his tongue—and she was on the verge of an explosion.

"You're so damn perfect." He nipped her inner thigh. "So mine."

She shuddered as his words washed over her. When she envisioned making love to Vaughn, she pictured hot and heavy, fast and hard. But this... his touch was so gentle she wanted to weep. At the same time, she wanted to beg him for more. She wanted to plead with him to hurry up and let her come.

Her heartbeat pounded in her ear when she felt his fingers brush against her core. She gasped when she felt his breath against her pussy. *Where the hell is my underwear?* He was so skilled she'd lost clothes without even knowing it. But she didn't have time to ask the question because his tongue circled her clit at the same time he pushed two fingers inside her. Emerie couldn't breathe, she couldn't think, she couldn't even remember her name because it was so good, so... *Oh God.* She was coming. Already. It took her over, drowning out everything but the delicious pleasure that spread through every inch of her body.

When she recovered, she opened her eyes and found him staring at her, his eyes dark. "You almost killed me with that," she told him.

"Oh, I'm not done eating." He smirked. "I just wanted you to catch your breath before I went back in for seconds."

"Vaughn," she breathed. "No, you don't—Oh. My. God."

He sucked her clit into his mouth. Her legs shook as the pressure of another delicious orgasm built within her. It didn't take long, and soon she cried out his name as she came against his tongue.

Vaughn kissed her there again, sending shockwaves through her. She gripped the short curls on his head. When he met her gaze again, she said, "don't even think about it."

"You're so bossy," he told her.

"I told you to come inside and I meant it."

He chuckled. "I plan to."

"Condom?" she asked.

Vaughn flashed the foil package at her. "Covered."

She sat up on her knees and helped him take off his clothes, allowing herself a moment to actually touch the muscles she couldn't get out of her mind the last few days. "You're so beautiful." She kissed his stomach, traced his muscles with her tongue.

She pushed his pants and underwear down, freeing his impressive erection. *Damn*. He was glorious. Every. Single. Inch. She stroked him, enjoying the way he growled her name. In that moment, she wanted to hear him say her name over and over as he took her, claimed her, possessed her.

Their mouths met in another kiss and he lowered her to the mattress. He searched her eyes, like he wanted to say something.

"What?" she asked, tracing the side of his face with her finger.

"You might destroy me."

Emerie's eyes widened. "Vaughn, I—"

He kissed her again, effectively cutting her off. In her twenty-eight years, she'd never been kissed quite like this. Tongue and teeth and hands everywhere. Vaughn put everything into it. He'd mastered the art of it.

"No more talking," he grumbled in her ear before he nipped her earlobe.

"Oh," she moaned. On any given day, if someone had told her ear play was sexy, she would have laughed in their face. But Vaughn had a way with her body.

He pressed his dick against her core, a question in his eyes. Nodding, she repeated her earlier words to him. "Come. Inside."

Vaughn slipped inside of her, filling her completely. *Oh damn.* They stayed like that for a moment.

"Shit," he breathed. "So tight."

Emerie bit his chin, urging him to move with her hips. He started slow, thrusting in and out. Eventually, he picked up the pace. Labored breathing, low moans, and soft grunts were the only sounds in the room as they moved together, pushing and pulling, giving and taking.

Vaughn hooked his arms under her legs, tilting her pelvis in such a way that made her delirious with desire. Her orgasm snuck up on her, pulling her over the edge. He followed her shortly after, sinking his teeth into her shoulder.

They lay still for a moment, each of them gasping for breath. Then, he rolled onto his back, pulling her with him. Emerie had never felt so loved, so satisfied, so spent after sex. The only thing she could do was rest her head against his chest as her body tried to recover to normal. Yet, even as she wrapped her arms around his waist, she knew nothing would ever be normal again.

He placed a kiss on her forehead. "Are you okay?"

A smile tugged at her lips, and she lifted her head. "Absolutely."

"I never expected this, Rie."

Perching her chin on his chest, she hummed. "Me neither. I did just break up with my boyfriend."

Bringing Marcus into this moment was a huge mistake. He didn't deserve to share the space with them. What she'd just shared with Vaughn meant more to her than anything she'd shared with her ex, which was very telling. The only question? *What does it mean to Vaughn?* He'd told her she could destroy him. But she didn't want to guess what that meant, because it could have meant anything.

Vaughn kissed her nose. "Like I told you, he didn't deserve you."

"Let's not talk about him." She cuddled into him. "I can't believe we just did this."

"I don't regret it," he said.

"You don't?"

"Rie, look at me." She hesitated, before lifting her head again. He brushed his thumb over her chin. "I wouldn't have done this if I wasn't sure. Being attracted to you is one thing, but not enough for me to risk my friendship with your brother for it."

Emerie's stomach clenched. "What are you saying?"

"I'm saying this isn't some random fling for me."

"Okay," she breathed. "So what do we do?"

"I don't know."

Emerie didn't know either. She didn't want to think about what Len would say when he found out. She knew her brother, and she knew Vaughn. There was no way he'd hide this new development from her brother. *But maybe he could…*

"Can we not tell Len for now?" she asked. Vaughn frowned, but she rushed on, "Just until we figure this out? I know you won't lie to him, and I don't want to do that either. Let's call it withholding the truth for now."

Vaughn stared at her, a slight frown on his face. "Do you really think he won't be able to tell?"

She let out a heavy sigh. "I know he will. But I don't want to have to explain this to anyone right now. And I don't want this to come between the two of you."

"If he asks, I won't lie to him. However, I won't volunteer the truth until we decide to do it together."

Nodding, she said, "I'm cool with that."

"Other than Len, what are you thinking?"

"Honestly?" Emerie didn't want to think about

anything or anybody else. They could talk about everything tomorrow. "I'm just wondering when we're going to do it again."

Vaughn wrapped his arms around Emerie. "Wake up, sleepyhead" He kissed her neck. They'd spent the night exploring each other in various positions. He'd lost control with her, and he didn't know how to get it back. Or if he wanted to.

Emerie let out a little sigh. "Vaughn." She stretched and pushed her behind into his morning erection.

He buried his face in her neck and slipped inside her. They made love quietly, slowly. Vaughn was fast becoming obsessed with her, the way she moved, the way she called his name, the way she felt beneath him or on top of him. There was something about the way they were with each other that filled a space within him that he thought was empty. And he didn't want to go back to how it was before this, before they'd crossed the line with each other.

"Vaughn," she whispered. "Yes."

His stomach quivered with the need to complete the act, but he couldn't come without her. He parted her slick folds, strummed her clit with his finger. She came with his name on her tongue, triggering his own release.

Seconds later, she turned and kissed him. "We should probably get up," she said. "We have the ball tonight. And you have sweated my hair out. I have to find Kerry."

She sat up on the edge of the bed and he smoothed a hand over her back. "Come with me."

Emerie glanced at him over her shoulder. "What?"

"Be my date to the ball."

"I don't know." She eyed him skeptically. "Are we ready for that?"

"It's a ball. We're both going, so it's not out of the realm of possibility that we'd ride together."

She sighed. "It's just… What if people ask questions?"

He perched himself up on his elbow. "What if they do?"

Vaughn wasn't sure why she was so hesitant about this. Or whether he was offended or hurt by her hesitation. Either one of those emotions made him the sap in this thing they had going on. Which was totally not normal for him. Usually, he was the one making up excuses to keep things on the low. And he'd made no apologies for his playa ways. Now, he actually wanted to be seen with a woman and she was the one acting unsure—or unbothered. *This sucks.*

Emerie stood and stretched. He loved that she wasn't shy around him, that she didn't try to hide her body from him. "Okay, Vaughn. I'll go with you tonight."

He rolled onto his back, staring at the ceiling. "Good."

Footsteps rounded the bed. "Are you mad?"

Raising a questioning brow, he asked, "Why would I be mad?"

She shrugged. "You just seem irritated."

With a sigh, he reached out and ran a thumb over one of her nipples. "I'm not." He let the back of his hand fall, brushing over her belly button and down to her pussy. Vaughn had never wanted a woman like this. It was all he could do to not pull her back in bed with him again. "You might want to get in the shower or you'll be back on this bed riding my dick."

Emerie winked. "I might be down for that." She walked to the door. "Or I could be in the shower riding you on the bench."

With that, she left the room. Part of him wanted to stay right where he was. But that was a very small part of him. Mostly, he wanted to spend as much time with her as possible. He wouldn't be in Michigan much longer, and he wasn't sure what they were doing.

Vaughn heard the shower turn on a few minutes later and decided to make the best of the situation. He hurried out of the bedroom to join her.

After they finished, he wrapped her in a towel. "When are you leaving?" she asked.

"Monday," he told her.

She combed her hair, meeting his gaze in the bathroom mirror. "Are you coming back here any time soon?"

Vaughn eyed her, curious about her question. "I wasn't planning on it."

"Oh," she said.

He rested his chin on her shoulder. "But I think things have changed."

A slow smile spread across her lips. "I think so, too."

"You could always come to L.A. to visit me."

"Maybe I will." She pulled her hair back into a pony-tail. "As long you give me a personal tour of your studio."

"I got you."

"Good." She kissed him. "Let's eat."

Vaughn wrapped his arms around her, smacked her ass. "I could eat."

She brushed her lips over his again, and they fell into a deep kiss. He backed her toward the bathroom door. The monotone voice of the security system announced that the alarm had been disarmed and the front door was open.

Emerie froze, her eyes wide and her mouth open.

"Shit," he said. "It has to be Len."

"Oh no," she whispered. "He's going to know we did it." Her gaze dropped. "Look at us."

He placed a finger over her mouth.

Len's voice rang out in the silence. "Rie?"

She glanced at the door, then back at him. "He saw my car," she mouthed.

"Answer him," Vaughn ordered.

Emerie sighed. "I'll be right out!"

"It's okay," he assured her. "Just go."

"This is your fault," she whisper-yelled, shaking her head. "This was a bad idea."

"Bad idea?"

"Not us." She motioned to the room. "This. Here." She paced the bathroom, shaking her head. "And we're in towels, after we had sex in his shower." She stomped to the door. "Len, I just got out of the shower. Can you go in the living room? I left my clothes in the bedroom."

They waited for Len to respond. It took a moment, but his best friend asked, "Is Vaughn in there with you?"

Emerie kicked at the air. "What?"

"Rie," Len said. "Answer the question."

Vaughn let out a heavy sigh. "Yes," he replied.

"I'm going to go outside for a few minutes and come back," Len said through the door. "Be dressed."

Fifteen minutes later, all three of them sat in the living room—Len on the recliner and Vaughn and Emerie on opposite ends of the couch.

"How did this happen?" Len asked.

Vaughn scratched the back of his head. "Do you want the honest answer?"

Len glared at him. "Of course. From Rie."

Yeah, his best friend was pissed. And Vaughn didn't blame him. While they'd never specifically banned dating siblings, Len knew too much about him to be comfortable with this latest development. The only way that would change was if Vaughn told Len the truth.

"I broke up with Marcus," Rie explained. "I came here to stay because I knew you were out of town. Vaughn was here and things happened."

"Dana told me about your breakup," Len said. "That's actually why I came back early. That, and I wanted to support Rhonda's ball."

"Len, it wasn't planned." Emerie crossed her legs at her ankles. "It happened and I'm okay with it."

"I'm not," Len said. "I don't think it's a good idea. At all."

Emerie stood. "Well, it's not really your choice. So…"

"You're right. It's not my choice. But you're my little sister. I'm concerned that you're rebounding with Vaughn."

Vaughn was concerned, too. That simple fact weighed heavy on him, but he'd tried to push past it. "Bruh, we're adults. Maybe we shouldn't have done this in your house. But I'm not sorry that it happened."

Len tilted his head, studying him, *seeing* him. They'd grown up together, so there wasn't much they didn't know about each other. Len had been there when his parents kicked him out, when he was arrested for smoking weed in the high school parking lot. He'd driven cross country with Vaughn when he moved to California. If his best friend had a serious problem with him seeing Emerie, it would definitely give Vaughn pause. Not that he would stop.

"Can we talk about this later?" Emerie asked. "I have to go see Kerry."

Vaughn grabbed her hand when she walked by him. "You okay?"

She nodded. "I'm fine. I'll see you later."

Once they were alone, Vaughn rested his elbows on his knees. "I'm sorry you had to find out this way, man."

"Vaughn, you know I trust you to do the right thing."

"I know," Vaughn said. "I don't plan on doing the wrong thing."

"Whatever happened between you and Rie is between you and her. But she's coming off of a long relationship. And you live in California. How is it going to work?"

The fact that Len seemed to be taking things well didn't make it any easier to explain to his friend why he'd done what he did. "We're not really defining it right now. It's just happening."

"And you're okay with that?"

Am I okay with it? It wasn't reasonable to expect anything more from her right now. She had a lot going on. It had only been a week since she'd broken up with Marcus. And they'd just slept together last night—and this morning. "I think I am."

Len laughed. "Whatever, bruh."

"Look, I'm not going to speak to that. The only thing I'm concerned with is letting you know I didn't make the decision lightly to be with her."

His best friend waved a hand at him. "That I *do* know about you."

Vaughn stood. "I'm going to head out and make some runs." He walked out of the room. That conversation went better than he expected. And he meant everything that he'd said. He didn't take this lightly. Now, he just had to convince Emerie.

Chapter 7

The Scholarship Ball was in full swing when Vaughn and Emerie arrived. They hadn't really spoken since Len had basically caught them in the act. Instead of discussing the implications, they'd done their own thing for the day. She'd spent most of the day out with Kerry while he'd stayed away, running errands for Rhonda.

The car ride to *Weber's Inn* had been relatively quiet, except for the small talk he'd forced himself to initiate. Vaughn was at a loss. She'd basically shut down on him, for whatever reason, and he wasn't sure how to break through the hard shell she'd erected.

He slid her a sideways glance. The black gown she wore was somehow classy, elegant, and sexy in equal measure. She was absolutely stunning, so beautiful he'd fought to keep his hands to himself.

As they approached the ballroom, she stopped, holding her hand out in front of him. Without a word, she gripped his arm and tugged him toward a little nook area around the corner.

Vaughn searched her eyes. "What's wrong?"

"We didn't talk about what happened earlier, and I think we should."

"Now?"

Emerie nodded. "I think it's important, yeah."

He checked the time. Rhonda had told him earlier that she'd deliver the keynote after dinner, which wasn't scheduled to be served for another half hour. Linking their fingers together, he led her to the registration desk and booked a room.

It took them several minutes to get to the penthouse suite. When they entered, he dropped the keycard on the table.

Emerie turned to him, one hand on her hip. "Don't you think this is weird?"

Vaughn sat on the couch. There was no time to talk in circles, so he asked, "I'm assuming you're talking about us?"

"Yes." She sighed and plopped down next to him.

He tried to focus on her and not the way she smelled or the way the slit in her dress fell open revealing her toned leg. Or the fuck-me stilettos she wore.

"Vaughn, you told me that we were crossing a line. Then, you told me I could destroy you."

Oh, that. He remembered saying it, but he'd tried to pretend he didn't. He should have known that she wouldn't forget. He scratched his upper lip and let out a heavy sigh.

"Before you say anything, let me just get this out," she said. "I'm not oblivious. I know this wasn't a random fling. I also know that we probably made a mistake jumping into bed so soon."

Vaughn shifted, suddenly uncomfortable with the conversation. "A mistake, huh?"

She placed her hand on top of his. "Not like that, Vaughn. I just meant the timing of it was off." Emerie closed her eyes. "I can't reconcile this sudden change in our relationship with everything I know about us. You've been in my life for so long. Too long to do something so drastic without thinking about the consequences. Or even what happens if this doesn't work. How am I supposed to look at you knowing you made me come fifty 'leven times in one night? When you go back to California, am I supposed to just forget about it? Go to work like my life hasn't changed? Do gigs like I can't remember your smell or the feel of your touch against my skin?"

Vaughn swallowed hard. "Rie, I—"

"Wait, because if I don't say this I might be convinced to never tell you how I feel."

He gestured for her to continue.

"Okay," she said. "I think we need to make a plan. A decision. Are we going to continue this, knowing it's practically impossible for this work? Or do we just cut our losses and try and salvage this lifelong friendship of ours?"

"Is that what you want?" He hoped it wasn't, but he needed to know. For the first time in his life, he wanted more. He wanted to take a chance and see where this would lead. Asking the hard questions now would save them time in the future.

Her shoulders fell. "No," she admitted. "But I also don't know what I'm doing with my life. I spent years with a man that I didn't want a lifetime with. I wasted valuable, precious time on something I knew wouldn't work out in the end. Don't ask me why because I can't really tell you. I can say that I'm tired of settling for less than I deserve. I'm tired of being the responsible, levelheaded woman afraid to really step out there and follow my dream. And I'm tired of pretending that you were ever big brother-like, that I ever felt familial about you. This might be new for you, but it's not for me."

Vaughn smiled. "That's good to hear."

"Is it? Because I don't want to get hurt again, Vaughn. Which is why I think we need to take a step back. Maybe slow things down?" He opened his mouth to argue with her, but she rushed on, "I don't know. You're going home Monday. I live here. I work here. My family is here."

As much as he hated to admit it, Emerie was talking hard facts. She'd laid out the things that he should have thought of before they started this. Still, he couldn't bring himself to admit it. Because now that he'd basked in her light, he didn't want to go back into darkness.

He dropped his head, hesitant to talk, to say anything that would ruin things. Maybe he could just pull her onto his lap and make love to her until she forgot about everything difficult.

He felt her fingers on his neck. "Vaughn, let's talk. Say something."

Glancing at her, he admitted, "Not sure what to say."

She ran her thumb over his cheek and kissed him. "Say that you don't regret this. Say that you understand what could happen if this doesn't work. I don't know, say that you want me."

"You can't see that I want you?" he asked. "I basically told my best friend to mind his damn business. Trust me, that was hard as hell. Especially since Len is *my* brother too. You're asking if I want you and I'm sitting here plotting a seduction to stop you from walking away from this, *from me.*"

"I'm not walking away."

He cradled her face and pulled her into a kiss. Leaning his forehead against hers, he whispered, "Don't."

That one word was all he could say. It somehow conveyed his desperation to keep her and his fear that this could end before it started. Vaughn had never believed in instant anything; not instant oatmeal, instant Jell-O, nor instalove. He wasn't stupid enough to believe he was in love with her. But he definitely was in something. Maybe it had been dormant inside of him for all these years, waiting for the right time to burst through his defenses and force him to feel it? Maybe every woman had been a stand-in for the one woman he thought he could never have or shouldn't even want?

"Should we talk about Monday?" he asked.

"Yeah," she replied with a wobbly smile. "Later. I don't want you to miss Rhonda's speech."

"We should probably go down," he said.

They made their way down to the ballroom. He heard the applause coming from inside and hoped he didn't miss Rhonda's speech. Opening the door, he stepped inside. Elijah was at the podium introducing Rhonda. He nodded and smiled at a few people who met his gaze. Then, he led Emerie to a table near the front, where Len, Dana and their family sat. Vaughn pulled out a chair and waited for Emerie to sit before he took his seat.

Smiling, he greeted the Cole family, ignoring their wide-eyed stares and open mouths. There would have to be a discussion with them, too.

Emerie glanced at him and squeezed his thigh. "We made it," she whispered.

He nodded. "We did."

The crowd stood, applauding Rhonda as she stepped up to the podium.

"Thank you for joining us tonight," Rhonda said, once everyone returned to their seats.

Vaughn winked at his sister when her gaze landed on him. She smiled.

"When I was younger, I found myself in a position that would change my worldview. I was pregnant, alone. And I was forced to make a decision. Did I want to bring this baby into a world that could care less about my struggle? Or did I want to bring my baby into a world that could be better? I chose to be the change I wanted to see for my baby, for my family. Before I continue, I want to give two very special thank yous. I want to thank my beautiful daughter, Elena, for forcing me to reach higher, to work harder, to love unconditionally. And I want to thank my brother, Vaughn, for riding with me through those tough first years, for standing in the gap when I needed him, for supporting me. It wasn't easy, but we made it work."

Vaughn's eyes burned with unshed tears. It didn't surprise him that his parents weren't in the room. They needed to be there to see the accomplished woman his big sister had become. They needed to be there to see that their lack of support hadn't stopped her from becoming a success.

Rhonda gave an inspiring speech on the importance of community and the need to for everyone to take the plight of our youth seriously. She thanked everyone important to her for their unwavering support. Then, she challenged everyone to get involved, to give back. Once again, the room applauded his sister, giving her a standing ovation.

When Rhonda stepped down from the podium, instead of joining her husband and children at their table, she approached him. "We did it," she whispered. "And it doesn't matter that they're not here. What matters is we are kicking some major ass out here." The emotion in her voice made him want to whisk her out of the room so they could have a private moment. "Don't ever let anyone tell you differently."

He pulled her into an embrace. "Never," he said.

The short program ended with him and Elena presenting an award to Rhonda that brought most of the room to tears—including him.

When he returned to the table, Emerie wasn't there. Minutes later, she returned with a drink and set it in front of him. "For you. Figured you might need that."

Vaughn glanced up at her. Her eyes were red, as if she'd been one of the many guests crying. He laughed. "You figured right."

Someone tapped his shoulder. He glanced up to see his youngest sister Roxanne standing there. "Roxy?"

She grinned. "Hi."

Standing, he pulled her into a hug. "I didn't expect to see you."

Vaughn hadn't seen his little sister in years. Not that he hadn't tried either. Roxy had been devoted to their parents from the beginning. She'd bathed in the Kool-Aid and had spent her life at the church her parents belonged to. When they turned their backs on him and Rhonda, she'd refused to place blame on them.

At times, he thought their relationship would never be repaired. But then she'd call him or email him just to let him know she was thinking about him. He learned from Rhonda that the two of them had even met for lunch several times.

"I couldn't miss it," she said, tears standing in her eyes. "I want to do better, big brother. I want to have a relationship with you."

It wasn't the first time she'd said this, but he wouldn't bring that up. He was just happy she'd come. "We can make that happen."

He eyed the man next to his sister, dressed in a plain black suit and bowtie. "Vaughn, this is Aiden. My fiancé."

Vaughn blinked. "You're getting married?"

"Yes, in June. I'd like you to be there."

He looked at Emerie, then at Len. They both knew how big this would be for him to voluntarily go to an event at the church that had made him feel like a second-class citizen. They both knew how seeing his parents would affect him. And they both nodded, offering silent support for whatever decision he made. Turning back to his sister, he nodded, "I'll be there. Send me the information."

She wrapped her arms around him. "I love you."

"Love you, too." He watched his baby sister walk away and hug Rhonda and her family. And he felt hope that things could be better between them for the first time in years.

Emerie squeezed his hand. "What an awesome moment!"

Vaughn nodded, emotion threatening to once again shatter his masculine image. Clearing his throat, he leaned down and whispered against her ear, "Want to finish our talk?"

She jerked her head back. "Now? The ball isn't over."

"Now."

Emerie stood and gave her family hugs.

"If I've never told you before, I'm telling you now… your life could have gone a different way, you could have let your circumstances minimize your success. But you didn't. Neither did Rhonda. I don't think I've ever been more proud to call you my family," Len said, giving him a quick hug.

"Thanks, bruh," Vaughn said. "I appreciate that."

"Good. I also feel like I have to make myself clear on one other thing."

Vaughn had a feeling he knew exactly what Len wanted to say, but he asked anyway, "What's that?"

"I will kick the shit out of you if you hurt my sister."

Vaughn barked out a laugh. "Alright, bruh. Whatever."

"I'm serious." Len glanced over at Emerie, who was talking to Dana. "I also want to tell you to be careful. Sometimes when two hurt people come together, no matter the circumstance, they spread and expand that hurt. It's not intentional, it's life."

Vaughn eyed his best friend. He knew Lennox was speaking from experience, given his last relationship. The African American Studies professor had experienced his fair share of loss as well. And Vaughn had dropped everything to support him. He expected no less from Len for him.

"Ready?" Emerie approached them.

Nodding, Vaughn gave Len some dap and said his goodbyes to his family. They decided to take advantage of the suite for the night, even though neither of them had brought a change of clothes.

Once they entered the room, she kicked off her heels and climbed into the bed. "What a crazy emotional day!"

Vaughn loosened his tie and pulled it off. He joined her on the bed. "Tell me about it." He rolled onto his back, staring up at the ceiling. "For some reason, I hoped my parents would show up. Which is surprising because they never have."

He felt her shift beside him, and knew she was looking at him. But he kept his gaze trained on the popcorn ceiling. Vaughn hated talking about his parents to anyone, even Rhonda, but he needed to get it out.

"When they kicked me out, I thought I was done," he explained. "I felt so abandoned. It's not a good feeling to be discarded by your parents. Yet, even though I know they're too brainwashed by that cult masquerading as a Baptist church, I've always hoped they'd come around. I always wanted them to come to me and tell me that they were wrong, that they followed my career, that they were proud of me... that they loved me."

Vaughn didn't consider himself a churchy person, but he believed in God. He knew that God was love. He figured out that the people running that organization had no grasp of God's love. They were all about condemnation and judgment. And he couldn't be a part of that, no matter how much his father had threatened him to fall in line or else. He'd chosen the "or else" when he started acting out, hanging with the wrong crowd, experimenting with drugs, and having sex with random girls and older women.

He still remembered the beating he'd received when he'd told his father he didn't want to belong to that particular church anymore. He still had the scar from the time the belt buckle cut his back. It had faded a little, but the memory was as vivid today as it was when he was thirteen years old.

Yet, even after all of that, after the hurt, after the disappointment, after the struggle, he still found himself looking toward the door. He still longed to see his mother's face or hear his father's voice.

"I can't imagine what you're going through," she said. "But you *are* loved, Vaughn. So many people admire you, respect you. People have modeled their careers after you, learned from you. The people who matter love you regardless of your past. We know that your mistakes do not define you. They molded you into the man you are today."

While Vaughn appreciated her encouraging words, he was stuck on the word "we".

We know that your mistakes do not define you. Which meant she included herself in the people who loved him. Although it wasn't a stretch given their history, the knowledge cracked his heart open and let her climb in and take up residence.

He looked at her then, struck by the compassion in her eyes. "You asked me if I wanted you earlier," he said, changing the subject.

"I did."

"Did you believe me when I told you I did?"

She swallowed visibly. "Yes," she whispered.

"Let me ask you, do you think that what we have is worth exploring?" Emerie averted her gaze, but he gripped her cheek, turning her to face him again. "We're supposed to be talking. Let's discuss this."

"I think what we have is scary. I don't want to hurt you and I don't want to be hurt."

"How about we don't go into this thinking that one or both of us will get hurt?"

"You live in California."

"With access to the airport."

She laughed. "Long distance relationships…" Emerie rested her head on his shoulder. "They don't work."

"Not true."

"Okay, we could try it. But the stretches of time between visits might make it hard to be faithful. You have women throwing themselves at you left and right, every day."

"I'm not going to lie, that's true. But I'd never cheat on you. If I say I'm with you, I'm with you. Period."

She ran her thumbnail over his collar. "I know myself, though. I get busy, your schedule is extremely packed with events. When would we find the time to see each other?"

"We could make it work. But if you don't think you can do this, say it. Rie, it's okay to just tell me."

"I want to," she admitted. "I want to spend time with you, getting to know you on this level. But I'd be lying if I said I wasn't afraid. Because I'm at this point in my life when I have to make some decisions about where I want to be."

"You could always come to Cali. You're between places right now. I have the contacts, the clout. If you want to expand your brand, I could help you."

Emerie pulled back, eyeing him skeptically. "Now you're asking me to move to L.A.?"

He shrugged. "Maybe that was a bit drastic, but now that I'm thinking about it, it's perfect. You could take the time you need to figure out what you want to do with your career."

"And live with you?"

"You don't have to live with me."

Emerie held his hand. "Vaughn, I appreciate the offer, but no. I can't move to L.A. for any reason other than my own choice. Besides, this is too new for me to take that chance. I hope you understand."

"I get it," he said. "Just letting you know that you have options. This isn't just about me and you. It's about you and your career."

She wrapped her arms around his waist and burrowed into him. "I'm glad you understand."

"We can take it one day at a time. Planned visits, phone calls, weekend getaways to a neutral setting."

"I can agree to that." She kissed his chest. "Slow."

"Hopefully not so slow that I have to wait to have your legs wrapped around me until the next time I see you."

Emerie laughed and sat up, lifting her dress and straddling his lap. "Is this better?"

He sat up, sliding his hands up her spine. "Perfect." Leaning in, he nipped her bottom lip before deepening the kiss. "More than perfect," he murmured against her mouth before he rolled her onto her back and showed her just how perfect they were together.

Chapter 8

*E*merie stared at the last text Vaughn had sent her, torn on how she'd respond. It wasn't a mean text. He'd never sent one of those. And it wasn't a dirty text. He'd sent plenty of those, which had led to hot phone sex on numerous occasions. It wasn't even a funny text. They'd sent GIFs, videos, memes, and other things to each other all day, every day.

It was just three simple words: *I miss you.*

Who knew those words would send her heart skipping over the edge of a cliff? Maybe simple wasn't the right word. *Simple* didn't describe what had happened between her and Vaughn over the last month and a half. It definitely didn't describe how she felt every time she heard his voice or saw his face flash across her screen. The emotions she felt—a combination of adoration, desire, and probably love—were anything but simple. They were complicated.

And she missed him, too. So much, she'd talked herself out of purchasing a ticket to Los Angeles several times in the last hour. They hadn't made promises for a lasting commitment, or forever, they'd only promised to communicate with each other no matter what. Now, he'd communicated with her and she couldn't stop thinking about it, about him.

"Girl!" Kerry snapped her fingers in Emerie's face. "Where are you, girlfriend?"

Emerie blinked. That's right, she was supposed to be having dinner with her sister and her best friend. Not overthinking a text. She stared at her bestie. "I'm here."

"Yeah, right," Kerry said. "You're in a daze and you have been since you got that text you've been staring at. I mean you have a perfectly good Patron Margarita over there that you have not touched."

Dana snatched Emerie's glass. "No worries. I'll take care of this." She took the straw out of Emerie's margarita and stuck her own in there. "Yum."

Emerie stared at her sister. "I really did want that."

Kerry snorted. "I can't tell. We had a whole conversation about Marcus walking in here with that ugly ass chick on his arm and you didn't even flinch.

Frowning, Emerie leaned forward. "Marcus is here?"

Dana nodded slowly. "Yeah, he's huddled up in a booth over there." She pointed toward the back of the restaurant. "Seriously, Rie, he walked right past us but your attention was squarely on that phone."

Emerie dipped a piece of shrimp into the cocktail sauce. "Well, good for him."

Kerry quirked a brow. "Straight up? That's all you have to say?"

"Yes." She ate her shrimp. It was rare that she got to go out to dinner with her faves. Their schedules didn't really allow for impromptu nights out. "I don't care what Marcus does."

"Damn, that's mature," Dana said. "If Lewis was in

this bar with another woman after he cheated on me, I might flip out."

Emerie laughed. "I hope you never go through that with Lewis, Dana."

Dana had been married to her high school sweetheart for ten-plus years and together for fifteen. Lewis doted on his wife and their daughters, and Emerie couldn't imagine him behaving anything like Marcus' ass.

"I hope Marcus is happy," Emerie said.

"Happy with the clap," Kerry muttered. "That's what his ass deserves."

Emerie laughed. "You're too much."

"Is Vaughn that good that you've magically forgotten how bad Marcus was?" Kerry asked. "Because after the way he behaved, I'd want to kick him in his face every time I saw him."

Buttering a roll, Emerie shook her head. "It's not that deep, Kerry. I don't care what he does or who he does it with."

Emerie didn't even try to see who Marcus was with. When she'd broken up with him, she was done. She didn't want to see him or hurl one last insult or sabotage any of his future relationships. It was over.

Dana gave Emerie a high five. "That's what I'm talking about. Go high when they go low."

"Shit, if they want to go low, I can get down in the gutter with them."

They broke out in a fit of giggles. "Crazy," Emerie muttered.

"So, I'm going to go out on a limb and guess that your text was from fine ass Vaughn." Kerry leaned forward and whispered, "Was he scheduling phone sex?"

Dana nudged Kerry. "Girl, you are too much."

"What?" Kerry asked with a shrug of her shoulders.

"I'm not getting any. I'm living vicariously through those who are."

Emerie took a sip of her water since Dana had guzzled down her alcoholic beverage. "No, he wasn't scheduling sex, fool. He said he missed me."

"Aw," Dana said, her hand on her heart. "He did? That's so freakin' cute."

"Forget cute. That's hot as hell."

Emerie thought it was both cute and hot. Too bad he wasn't around for her to make a booty call. *Who am I kidding?* Nothing about them screamed booty call. From the beginning, they'd connected on a deeper level.

"What if I—?"

Kerry held up a hand. "Stop. I know what you're doing. All I have to say is life is too short to not grab hold of love when you can, when it's real."

"Who said I was in love with him?"

Dana made a face. "Are we playing this game, sis?"

Emerie's mouth fell open.

"Close your mouth, girlfriend," Kerry said. "You don't have to do this with us."

"We've only been talking for a little over a month," Emerie argued. "Key word—talking. I've seen him once since he went to back to L.A."

And that one night had provided a bunch of heated memories. They'd met in Houston for one of his shows. After he performed for a crowded stadium, he'd taken her to his luxury suite and they didn't come out until it was time for her to go to the airport.

"So you have to do something about that," Dana said. "Obviously, you miss him, too. Go see him. Matter of fact..." She picked up her phone and typed something. A moment later, she said, "Flights are less than $400 right now." She held up her phone and Emerie read the flight information. "I can grab this one for you. I still have your rewards login information from that trip to Jamaica last year."

"No," Emerie said. "You don't have to get my flight. I'm not going to L.A. tonight or tomorrow. Besides, I'll see him in a couple weeks."

Emerie applied for a gig at the huge Chi-Flavor Afro-Caribbean Carnivale in Chicago this July, and had scheduled a meeting with the organizers. Vaughn had also been contracted as a featured DJ for the festival and had offered to meet her there and introduce her to a promoter he'd been working with for years.

Kerry finished her martini. "A couple of weeks is a long ass time when you're sexually frustrated. Trust me, I know."

"Don't we all," Dana agreed.

"I went six months without sex in my relationship. I can last a few more weeks."

"Sheeiiitt," Kerry muttered. "Whatever."

"Besides, I don't want to get into a habit of needing him. A little distance might be healthy for us right now."

Dana let out a dramatic sigh. "Rie, I'm your sister and I love you. I want you to be happy. As much as it pains me to say this, I have no choice. Get off your ass and get your shit together. You're thinking too much about this."

"Right," Kerry said. "Vaughn is not Marcus. He's not sending dick pics to random women online, is he?"

"I don't think so," Emerie said.

Of course, she didn't know for sure that he wasn't sending pics of his peen to anyone. But her heart told he wasn't. Her heart actually trusted him. Now, if she could get her brain there, she might be able to make a decision.

"Then, go for it," Dana said. "Take your behind to L.A."

"What if this is too good to be true?"

Her sister reached across the table and squeezed her hand. "You'll never know if you don't step out there. Have you talked to Len?"

"No."

"You're staying there," Dana said. "Why haven't talked to him about it?"

"He's my brother. I don't talk to him about my relationships."

"Len gives good advice. I talked to him about Lewis and he told to follow my heart and gave me his blessing. We're still happily married today."

"And he told me to leave my trifling ass husband," Kerry added. "He was right."

Emerie chuckled. "I'll think about it. That's the best I can do for now."

"Don't think too long," Kerry said. "I'm just sayin'. As you know, time is a precious commodity."

Later, Emerie walked into Len's condo. "Hey," she greeted, walking over to the couch where he was watching TV.

"What's up, Rie?" Her brother paused the show he was watching. "You're home early."

"Yeah, I'm tired. I need to get some sleep."

The ladies had given her a lot to think about earlier. Flying to L.A. was appealing on so many levels, but what if she didn't come back right away. It wasn't like she had a home yet. She'd worked with her realtor to find a place and hadn't seen anything she liked.

Len had been gracious enough to let her stay with him, but she couldn't live there forever. She didn't want to stay with her brother anyway. At this point, she wasn't sure she wanted to stay in Michigan. *But is L.A. my ultimate destination?*

Moving to L.A. was a gamble. Did she really want to live with another man who could just kick her out when he felt like it or got tired of her? The answer to that was a resounding hell no. Vaughn wasn't Marcus, though. Despite her reservations, she couldn't find a reason not to trust him. He'd been honest with her from the beginning. Now, could she be honest with him?

"Len, I need to talk." She sat next to her brother. "I need some advice."

Her brother glanced at her, a frown on his face. "Are you okay?"

"I'm good. I just… Something happened."

"What?"

"I fell in love," she admitted softly.

Len smiled. "Is that a good thing?"

She nodded. "I hope so. I just want to know what you think."

"Why does it matter?" he asked.

"Because you know us both. You observe. You watch. And your opinion does matter."

Len hugged her. "You know what I think?" He rested his chin on her head. "I think you already know the answer. You're just trying to talk yourself out of it because you're scared."

She pulled back. "Maybe. But can you just say the words?"

He laughed. "If you need them. I think if you love him, then you need to tell him."

"What if he…?" She stared straight ahead, at the tiny sun on one of her brother's paintings. "What if it doesn't work?" She let out a shaky breath.

"What if it does?" Len asked.

Emerie met her brother's gaze. "Because it might work, right?"

"I'd say it's a high probability that it will. And I wouldn't tell you that, if I didn't believe it."

She wondered what made her brother so confident. Did Vaughn talk to him about it? "You wouldn't."

"So, here are the words… I approve. Now, what are you going to do with them?"

Len's blessing made her next words easier to say. "I'm thinking of a cross country move."

———

Emerie knocked on the heavy oak door. She'd booked her flight right after she talked to Len. Then, he'd driven her to the airport first thing in the morning. It was early and she was taking a chance by surprising him like this, but she had to see him.

A moment later, the door swung open. "Rie? What are you—?"

She cut him off with a kiss. It felt so good to be in his arms again, she didn't want to let go. Vaughn pulled her to him, deepening the kiss. *Oh God.* She'd missed this. She missed his lips on hers, his body against hers.

Without warning, he lifted her in his arms and carried her into the house. He pinned her against the wall, trailing kisses along her jaw to her ear. "You're here."

Emerie couldn't catch her breath. She wanted to talk to him, but she also wanted to come. She also didn't want her luggage just sitting outside on the porch.

She pulled back. "Vaughn, wait." He brushed his mouth over her chin, down her neck. "Oh my," she whispered, ready to give in, but knowing she couldn't. "My luggage."

He stopped kissing her and met her gaze. "It's outside?"

She nodded. "You pulled me in before I could tell you."

Vaughn smirked. "You started it." He let her go, setting her on her feet. He disappeared out of the door and came back seconds later with her suitcases. "How long are you staying?"

Emerie bit her lip. "Can we talk?"

"Of course."

She grabbed his hand and pulled him further into the house. Emerie immediately fell in love with the place—the windows, the art, the furniture, the walls. It was Vaughn. But it could be her, too. "You have a nice house."

"It's alright," he said.

Emerie plopped down on the couch. "Can you sit?"

"You're so bossy." He sat next to her. "Thirsty?"

She shook her head. "I could drink something." A shot of tequila might be good. "Water?"

Vaughn left the room, returning moments later with two bottles of water. He handed her one and sat back down. "I can't believe you're here."

"About that." She twisted the cap off of her bottle and gulped it down. Once it was gone, she set the empty bottle on a table. "I felt like we should talk."

"And you flew all the way here?"

"I did. You sent me a text last night."

Vaughn's gaze softened and he traced the line of her nose with his fingers. "You didn't respond."

"I figured it might be better if I responded in person."

He smirked. "When you just could have sent me a text letting me know you missed me too?"

"Exactly. I wanted to tell you to your face."

"Okay."

"I miss you," she said. "I miss you so much I couldn't go another day without seeing you."

Vaughn cupped her cheek. "That's good to hear," he whispered.

"You know what else is good?" She searched his eyes. "I'm 99.999 percent sure that I'm in love with you."

He chuckled and the sound shot straight to her core, reminding her that it was time to get this show on the road so she could get good sex. "I can't get a hundred percent? Because I'm one hundred percent sure I'm in love with you."

Emerie's mouth fell open, but he tipped her chin up, closing it. "You are?"

"Oh, yeah."

"Is this weird?"

Vaughn shook his head. "Not at all."

"Okay. So, yeah, I'm in love with you. And I just think that if we're going to do this, we should be in the same city."

His eyes widened. "Are you moving here?"

"I don't know. I just know it won't work if we're not with each other, if we don't see each other. So, I'm not actually saying that I'm moving in with you or even permanently moving to L.A. Yet. But I did take a leave of absence from my job and I want to give this a shot. It might be foolish, it might be fast, but it's definitely worth the risk."

"Rie, I don't know what to say."

"Say something. Say yes. Say you can't live another day without me. Say you love me so much you can't imagine being with anyone else. Tell me you want me."

Vaughn kissed her hard. "Yes, I can't live another day without you. I love you so much I can't imagine being with anyone else. I want you. I always want you. I'll always want you."

Tears spilled from her eyes, streaking down her face. "Oh shit, you said it. You really did that."

Vaughn laughed. "And I'll do it forever. Any time you want me to."

She wrapped her arms around his neck. "Good. Vaughn?"

"Yes?"

"You can take me to bed now."

Vaughn stood, scooping her up in his arms. "Oh, that was a given."

"Love you," she murmured against his lips.

"Love you, too."

Epilogue

*T*hree months later

Northerly Island, along Lake Michigan, was a beautiful setting for the Chi-Flavor Afro-Caribbean Carnivale. Emerie and Vaughn strolled through the crowd, stopping at vendor tables, sampling food, and checking out the various bands and dance groups in attendance.

Emerie loved the atmosphere, the spirit of community among the attendees. The music—a mixture of Afro Beats, Reggae, Hip Hop, and Rhythm & Blues—was the best part of the event for her. The live bands, the musical artists on the stage, and the DJs were off-the-chain lit. She couldn't wait to get up there and do her thing in a few hours.

They'd planned for a full day at the festival but missed the Saturday morning parade because they were otherwise occupied… in bed.

It was Vaughn's fault, Emerie thought. He was so damn irresistible, she couldn't tell him no. She didn't *want* to tell him no.

They'd landed at O'Hare Airport Friday afternoon,

drove to a Garrett Popcorn Shop to pick up her favorite Chicago Mix, and checked in to their Magnificent Mile hotel. The plan was to go to a dinner and make an appearance at a popular nightspot, but her boyfriend decided he'd rather stay in… naked.

One of the things she loved about Vaughn was his insistence that they spend time together, doing nothing but just sitting in each other's presence. Sometimes they talked, sometimes they were quiet, sometimes they cuddled, and sometimes they played cards or board games. Most times, they ended up naked. And Emerie didn't mind at all.

"Check this out." Vaughn pulled her over to an artist selling paintings. "This is cool as hell." It was an abstract piece, expressing the relationship between house music and hip hop.

"You should get it," she told him. "It would be perfect in your studio."

He glanced at her. "Think so?"

"Definitely."

Vaughn studied the image for a few more minutes, while she browsed the full collection. He wrapped his arm around her waist, pulling her to him. "I'm going to get it."

She leaned up on her the tips of her toes and kissed his jaw. "Do it."

"Nah," he said a moment later. "How the hell am I going to get it home? Let's go." He thanked the artist and they headed toward the food truck she'd pointed out earlier.

While he ordered their food, Emerie told him she had to go to the restroom and doubled back to the vendor. Since Vaughn's birthday was next month, she purchased the painting for him. Then, she made arrangements for Kerry—who'd driven to Chicago for the festival—to pick it up.

When she rejoined her boyfriend, he handed her a plate of jerk chicken. "Thanks," she said. "Want to sit?"

"We can keep moving," he said.

They arrived at the stage a while later. "Ready?" he asked.

"I'm so nervous," she confessed. "What if I suck?"

He kissed her temple. "You won't. You never do. You're kicking ass out here. All day, every day."

Since she'd moved to California, she'd booked several high-profile jobs, produced a song for a popular R&B artist, and even hired a manager to help advance her career. And Vaughn had never failed to support her.

"You got this," he added.

She beamed. "I do, don't I?"

"Yep. Get your ass up there and work the crowd."

"I'm going, I'm going." She kissed him. "I love you, baby."

He smacked her ass lightly. "Love you, too."

Five minutes later, Emerie was on stage doing what she loved. The music flowed, the crowd was hype, and she was on cloud nine. Halfway through her mix, she slid a glance to the side of the stage. Vaughn stood, his hands in his pockets and his head bobbing to the beat. He grinned at her and patted his heart.

It was his thing. He'd told her that she owned his heart, and he never let her forget it. She looked down at her hand, loving the way the diamond on her left ring finger sparkled in the sunlight. Oh, he'd proposed last night, too… naked. Emerie didn't hesitate, even a little bit. She couldn't wait to be Mrs. Carr.

Emerie had gone to L.A., not knowing what the future held, and ended up staying. It was the best decision she could have made. Now, she had the best of both worlds, a good part-time job at Cedars-Sinai Hospital that allowed her the flexibility to work on her passion. But the cherry on top was Vaughn—her man, her love.

*I*f Paityn could ban two words, *fuck* and *shit* would be it. One made her think of toilets. The other? Well, let's just say she didn't need to be reminded of something she hadn't been blessed to do in years. And for the last ten minutes, she'd listened to her sister string those same two words together in varying combinations.

"Girl! Enough!" Paityn shouted, cutting her sister off mid-curse. "Road rage is really a thing. Get help." Pulling two sets of new sheets out of the dryer, she walked into one of the spare bedrooms and dropped the bedding on the mattress.

"Shit, I need to vent," Blake yelled. "It's your fuckin' fault I'm in this predicament. Michigan traffic doesn't make me want to kill someone."

Unable to help herself, Paityn giggled at her younger sister's antics. "You're a mess."

"Hey, I can only be me," Blake said.

The loud blare of the car horn followed by another colorful curse had her shaking her head in amusement. Some things would never change. Trump was still an asshole, she still couldn't eat beans to save her life, and Blake Young still had a potty mouth.

"I'm hanging up," Paityn told her sister. "I have stuff to do before you get here."

When "the brats" told her they were coming for a visit during the Memorial Day holiday, Paityn was ecstatic. Since her cross-country move, she'd seen her sisters countless times thanks to technology. But air kisses and virtual hugs didn't replace real face-to-face contact.

"Paityn?" Bliss called through the phone. She noted the rasp in her baby sister's voice, as if she'd been sleeping. "Are you making something for dinner? I'm hungry."

"Yes, ma'am." She walked the other set of sheets to the third bedroom and dumped them on the bed. "I'm making reservations. At this new Cuban restaurant Rissa told me about."

"Damn," Bliss muttered. "Will you at least cook breakfast in the morning?"

"You're so greedy," Blake said. "You just ate a whole foot-long sub and half of mine."

"I can't help it," Bliss shouted.

"I'm starting to think you're only here because you want me to cook for you." Paityn hurried to the kitchen and opened the oven. The homemade peach cobbler she'd prepared was almost done, Blake's favorite.

"No, I'm here because I miss you," Bliss said, just as Blake shouted another obscenity at a driver.

"That's good to hear." She also checked the macaroni and cheese baking in the bottom oven. *My favorite.*

"I wish Dallas could have come," Bliss mused. "I tried to get her to cancel her plans."

Paityn lifted the top off the pot on the stovetop, stirring the mustard and turnip greens a bit before she turned down the heat. "I do, too. But I'm not mad at her for taking a vacation out of the country. It's about time." She glanced at the Instant Pot on the countertop, noting the remaining time on the pulled pork, Bliss' favorite.

The truth? She did have reservations for dinner and dancing. Tomorrow. But, tonight, she also wanted to spoil her sisters a little. And it had been a while since she'd cooked anything of substance.

Growing up the second oldest child of a world-renowned couple, known for mending relationships and teaching others to parent, had a unique set of challenges. Partly because it was hard to live in her parents' shadows, but mostly because there were eight of them. Yes, Stewart and Victoria Young had eight damn children—willingly and happily. Paityn was the responsible sister, the oldest daughter, always offering a plate of food, a hand to hold, and a shoulder to cry on.

"Duke is pissed you didn't invite him," Bliss said.

Paityn laughed, thinking of the phone call she'd received from her brother earlier that morning. "I didn't invite y'all."

"But you're glad we're here," Blake added.

"I am, but I'm hanging up. I gave the concierge your names, so you should be able to come up without any problems. Don't kill anybody, Blake. See you soon."

Paityn ended the call after her sisters screamed good-bye. Shaking her head, she turned the dishwasher on and poured a glass of wine. When the oven timer went off, she pulled the dessert out and set it atop the island. The smell of peaches and cinnamon wafted to her nose and she resisted the urge to taste the cobbler.

She scanned the notes she'd jotted down earlier that day. The clitoral cream she'd hoped to perfect had been harder than she originally thought. Between her work as a sex therapist and her science background, it should have been a no brainer. Yet, she'd failed to even achieve the big "O" for the first two batches she'd made. Biting her thumbnail, she pondered her choice of ingredients. Maybe she'd used too much sodium benzoate?

Paityn scribbled an idea on the notepad and eyed the prototype she'd created. It was the fifth dildo she'd created and, by far, the best. She couldn't wait to show Blake and Bliss, which was why it was out in the open and not in her makeshift office-slash-lab.

Once Paityn had decided every woman needed a big ass dick, the wheels started spinning and a business idea formed. Paityn knew there were other sex aids on the market, entire stores dedicated to the business of pleasure, but she'd jumped in anyway. Now she was preparing to pitch her brand of sexual enhancement products.

When her stomach growled, Paityn glanced over at the peach cobbler. *One spoonful won't hurt.* She grabbed a wooden spoon and scooped a heaping helping out of the pan. Before she knew it one bite turned into two. Then, three. *Oh my God.* Four.

Fortunately, the knock on the door interrupted her greedy moment. She licked the spoon as she headed toward the door. She'd figured it would be at least thirty minutes before her sisters arrived. The airport was less than fifteen miles away, but it almost always took more than thirty minutes to get there in the infuriating 405 traffic.

She wiped a hand against her black leggings and opened the door. "You're her—"

Only it wasn't Blake or Bliss at the door. It wasn't even Rissa. No, the very *male* visitor standing there, his fist poised to knock again, was someone she didn't know. But damn, he was someone she probably *should* get to know.

Swallowing, she plastered a grin on her face and hoped

she looked presentable. "Hi." When he didn't answer immediately, she swallowed. *Maybe the hottie is a creeper?* But it wasn't like she was in some random apartment building. The concierge didn't just let anyone come up to the top floor.

The stranger's eyes dropped to her mouth and she absently wiped it with her sleeve, hoping she didn't have peach cobbler crust on her face.

"Can I help you?" she asked.

He blinked and then blessed her with the sexiest smile she'd ever seen up close. Pretty white teeth, adorably deep dimples, and beautiful creases framing full lips.

"I'm sorry. My name is Bishop." He held out a hand, presumably for her to shake it.

Her gaze dropped to it, noted his long fingers and clean fingernails, but she made no move to touch him. *Not yet*.

"I work at Pure Talent," he continued. "Jax Starks told me about you."

Paityn's eyes widened. "Oh, yeah. Bishop Lang."

Why is my voice so high? Probably because when her godfather told her he wanted her to meet one of the best legal minds on his team, she'd assumed it was an old, graying grandfather. A man that golfed on his off days and spent weekends at some highbrow country club drinking Burnt Martinis or scotch on the rocks. Not this fine ass man with smooth dark skin and a body that made her want to sing, "Do me, Baby". Because she was sure he'd be able to handle the job in a way no one ever had before. *Focus, Paityn*.

"Yes, that's me." His tongue darted out to wet his lips. "I live in the building and figured I'd come up and introduce myself."

Unable to turn away, she nodded. "Right. I think Uncle Jax did tell me that."

Briefly, she wondered if this was even a good idea, considering she couldn't stop staring at him. How would she be able to concentrate on business? But she trusted her godfather's judgment because he had never failed her and always had her best interests at heart.

From an early age, Paityn learned that blood didn't make family. And it was because of relationships like the one her father and Jax Starks had. The two men had grown up near each other in Detroit, Michigan and had even pledged the same fraternity. They were brothers in every sense of the word, even though they were born to different parents. Jax was her godfather, but he was also her "uncle".

She finally stepped aside. "Come in."

He followed her toward the kitchen. "Peach cobbler." The low groan that followed hit her right in the gut—or lower. "Smells good."

She gulped down the rest of her wine and dropped the wooden spoon into the sink. "I'm making dinner for my sisters." She turned the greens off and tried to recall everything her godfather had told her about Bishop. Clearly, she'd missed some things that he'd said. "I thought you were going to be out of town until next week?"

"I got back a little early."

Paityn leaned against the counter, meeting his intense gaze once again. "Cobbler?" she asked.

He looked down at the dessert and swallowed visibly. Nodding slowly, he said, "No."

Paityn frowned, surprised at his answer. Normally, a nod meant yes. "You sure? Because you look like you want some."

"I'm sure." He glanced at the pan again, before he looked up at her.

Tilting her head, she studied him. Something was preventing him from eating her cobbler. Did she want to know what? *Or who?* The need to know more welled up inside her. *It's the nature of my job to ask questions.* It wasn't his arms. Or the muscles stretching against the t-shirt he wore. The fact that he may be eating someone else's pie didn't bother her either. Well, not really.

Instead of probing further, she decided a change of subject was best. "Uncle Jax tells me you work in the business development department," she said. "But what else should I know?" Okay, so her attempt to sound professional came out more sultry than businesslike.

"What do mean?" he asked.

Clearing her throat, she added, "Because if we're going to work together, I'd like to learn a little more about your ass." Her eyes widened. "I mean, your experience?"

He chuckled. "I can give you the long version, or the short version."

Hello, sexual innuendo. She really did need to get some. Everything about this man and this interaction made her mind sink to the gutter. Paityn scratched her neck. "How about we start with where you're from?"

"Long Beach."

She opened the refrigerator and pulled out two bottles of water and offered him one. "Law school?"

"Berkeley." He took the water and twisted off the cap. "I've worked for the agency for fifteen years, and I've been instrumental in negotiating several business deals for agency clients. Jax has also entrusted me with many of his personal business matters."

"Good. What has he told you about me?"

His mouth curved into a smile. "He mentioned you were important to him and that I should take care of you."

She bit down on her lip. "I mean, about my business idea."

"Only that you were a sex therapist looking to start a new venture."

Paityn grinned, pleased that he didn't seem uncomfortable with her occupation like some men. "That's true. Did he tell you anything else?"

Bishop raised a brow. "No. I assume you will tell me the details."

"Right. I'll send you the draft of my proposal." She slid her notebook over and jotted down a note to herself. "I probably should have done this as soon as he gave me your email address, but I didn't want to interrupt your vacation. I know we always say we won't check emails on vacation, but we always do."

Ha barked out a laugh. "I don't disagree with that."

"Let me know when you're free to meet." She closed the notebook. "I have appointments during the day, but I'm usually free in the evenings." Paityn conducted her sessions online, via video chat or text therapy, which she'd found to be a great alternative to in-office therapy. Most of her clients loved the convenience and it allowed her to work from the comfort of her home, wherever that was.

"I'll check my calendar and get back to you. I have your numbers."

"Great. You'll have an email tonight. Not that I don't think you wouldn't read my proposal before we meet, but you definitely should. And preferably not in the office. In front of people."

The last thing she wanted was for a picture of her prototype to flash across his screen while he had someone in his office. That would be embarrassing, for him and for her.

Bishop frowned. "Why do I feel like I should be scared?"

Paityn laughed. "Because you should." She waggled her eyebrows.

"Now, I'm curious. Maybe you should give me a hint?"

"I would, but—" A knock on the door interrupted her explanation. "Excuse me. I have to get the door."

She ran to the door and opened it. Before she could say anything, Blake and Bliss surrounded her, hugging her tightly. Paityn wasn't overly emotional, but it felt good to hug her sisters, and she held on for longer than normal.

Finally pulling back, she smiled at the twins, noting the tears standing in Bliss' eyes. She brushed her cheek. "Don't cry."

"Please don't." Blake rolled her eyes. "It hasn't even been a month. Get it together."

"Leave me alone." Bliss elbowed Blake. "At least I don't have a black heart."

Paityn giggled. "Get in here." She pulled one of the rolling suitcases inside. "Are you hungry?"

Bliss patted her stomach. "You know it."

"I thought you weren't cooking," Blake said.

Paityn led them around the corner into the open living room area. "You know I wasn't going to let you come here without making your favorites."

"So, no Cuban food?" Blake asked. "Because I had my mouth set… Oooh wee. This place is gorgeous. Floor-to-ceiling windows, stunning artwork. And I love the color scheme. Everything just flows. Uncle Jax is doing big things."

Bishop glanced up from his phone and stood. "Hi."

Blake bit down on her thumbnail. "And apparently so are you," she muttered under her breath.

"Who is that, sissy?" Bliss whispered.

"And tell me he has a brother," Blake added.

Paityn rolled her eyes. "Shut up." She introduced them to Bishop. "He's an attorney at Pure Talent and he's helping me with my business."

"Oh, so you're helping her with the Big Ass D?" Blake asked, a wicked gleam in her eyes.

Bishop blinked. "Excuse me?"

Paityn glared at Blake. "He doesn't know about that yet," she said between clenched teeth. Leave it to her little sister to embarrass the hell out of her. "I'm sorry, Bishop. Don't mind her."

"Is that peach cobbler?" Blake asked.

"Yes," Bliss answered from the kitchen. She lifted the top off the pan. "And there's greens. And it smells like pulled pork. Yum."

Paityn shrugged when Bishop met her eyes. "Sisters."

"Right," he said. "I should probably get going, let you visit with your sisters. We'll talk."

"I'll walk you out."

He waved her off. "You don't have to."

"I do." Paityn walked him to the door. "Thanks for stopping by. I'm looking forward to working with you." She finally reached out to shake his hand.

When their palms met, she couldn't help but notice how the contact flooded her with warmth, from the tips of her fingers to her shoulders and throughout her body.

"It's good to meet you, Paityn." His husky, low voice made her want to lean into him.

She didn't, though. Slipping her hand from his, she nodded. "Right."

"I'll talk to you soon."

She nodded again. Because apparently she couldn't form any words.

Once he was safely outside the door, she exhaled. If every interaction with him ended with a handshake that somehow felt more like a kiss or a tender caress against her bare skin… *I'm definitely in trouble.*

Excerpt: The Closing Bid
DISTINGUISHED GENTLEMEN SERIES

*T*he cold didn't reach his bones. It never did out there. The smell of peanuts and grass, the sound of wood cracking against leather, the roar of the crowd, the feel of the dirt underneath him... it all felt like home to him. The field was his safe place, one of only a handful of safe places in his life.

Christian Knight had spent years building a career as a professional baseball player for the Detroit Jaguars. He was bigger than life there, an integral piece to an important puzzle, and one of the best "closers" in the league. And in a few weeks, he would be stepping on the mound for opening day one last time. The upcoming season would be his final one.

Life for him hadn't been all that easy lately, starting with the discovery of his ex-wife having an affair without regard for his feelings. Having a marriage deteriorate in the public eye should have been the worst thing that he'd ever experience. Finding out about the affair in the pages of a magazine could have stolen that honor. But, no, it was the sudden death of his mother that had Christian questioning everything about his life.

He turned, surveying the empty ballpark. In half an hour, he'd announce his retirement to the world. The decision to end his career so soon had thrown the team into a lurch, but he couldn't imagine staying another year. Because he wasn't the same person who'd vowed to play until he couldn't walk anymore. Baseball didn't define him anymore.

Christian heard the sound of footsteps on grass nearing him and turned. His entertainment attorney, Zara Reid, approached him, a smile on her face. Everything about her commanded respect, from her sensible but sexy suit to her "power pumps" as she called her heels. As always, she looked ready to wheel and deal in a black pencil skirt, silk blouse, and lightweight jacket. Her long hair was pulled back into a neat ponytail and she wore little to no makeup on her smooth brown skin.

He'd been with Zara for five years, and she'd done more for him in that time than his first two agents. Endorsements were rolling in, with everyone from fashion designers to shoe companies to fast-food chains. When he'd signed with her, she'd told him that she worked for him, and assured him that she would fight hard for him. So far, she'd never let him down, proving herself as his strongest advocate time and time again.

"Are you ready?"

He sighed and stuffed his hands into the pockets of his dress pants. If it were up to him, he would have worn jeans and a t-shirt. But Zara had suggested he look a little more "put together". He chuckled when Zara muttered a curse about dirt on her Manolo Blahniks.

"Shit, it's cold as hell out here."

"It's March. In Michigan." He shook his head at her

outfit. "Maybe next time wear a coat?" He paused. "I don't want to take a lot of questions," he said. "Two, maybe three."

Zara sighed. "How about five? This is a big deal. You're not only retiring, but your announcing your new mentorship program. We want to make sure your fans know you're not going away completely."

Christian held up one hand, indicating five questions were okay.

"Two things—this press conference is going to blow my phone up with requests for interviews. It will also open you up to questions about non-baseball things. And I need you to keep your cool."

He glared at his agent. "I always keep my cool."

Zara sighed heavily. "Under normal circumstances." She squeezed his arm. "Christian, you've had so much to deal with in the last year. Your emotions are raw. Don't assume they won't bring up Meena."

Hearing his ex-wife's name only served to heighten his emotions. The melancholy he'd felt when the plane landed earlier that morning at the Detroit Metropolitan Airport ebbed a little when he'd stepped out on the field, but now... The last thing he wanted was a rehash of the hell he'd been through over the past several months.

Christian hated the press, had rarely granted interviews because he valued his privacy. He didn't post on Facebook, he rarely tweeted, didn't even know how to SnapChat, and didn't take selfies or pictures of his food to post on Instagram. When he granted interviews, there was always a bigger purpose—new contract negotiations, community support for much needed programs, or after-game impressions. That's it. Even then, he didn't like the questions, the lights, the intrusion into his private life.

He'd tried his best to stay out of the tabloids during his

career. He had a reputation for being a stand-up man—someone who honored his commitments, someone who gave back to his community for all the right reasons, and someone who didn't do things for "likes" or "retweets". All of that changed last summer, during the height of the season. But it wasn't because of anything he'd done. It was all on Meena—and the journalist who'd exposed the prostitution ring his wife had been involved in. Which, in turn, revealed the torrid affair she'd been having with the General Manager of one of his rival teams.

"Christian?" Zara peered up at him, concern in her brown eyes. "I just it's best to be prepared for the worst."

"I'm fine. *If* they bring up Meena, I'll politely deflect."

His agent shot him a disbelieving look, then waved a hand of dismissal in his direction. "Fine. About the interviews… it's your ball game. Pun intended. You tell me how many you want to do."

The answer to that was easy. Zero. But he knew going into this that was impossible. So, he threw out the next best number. "One."

Her eyes widened. "One? What the hell? Christian, give me something to work with. I'm trying to set you up for your after-baseball money. I can't do that if you continue to play coy with reporters."

Shrugging, he said, "We've already had this discussion multiple times since I told you I was done with the game. Aside from a few endorsements, I'm okay not doing commentary or staying involved in the politics of the league. Hence, the reason why I'm retiring."

Zara rolled her eyes. Hard. "Fine. I'm going to have to fire you."

Christian laughed. "Fire me? Isn't that backwards. You work for me, so technically, wouldn't I have to let you go?"

"Whatever. I only get paid when I work. Which means, I need to wheel and deal for you."

He shook his head, still chuckling at his friend. "Do you threaten to fire all of your clients? Or just me?"

"Just you. You're the only one I call friend." Zara cleared her throat.

They'd discussed her role in his career once he actually retired and had both agreed that she would continue to do what he needed her to do, whether it was a lot or a little. But she had earned a permanent spot on his life's journey because she'd been a good friend to him. That would never change. "We'll talk about this later. You good?"

Nodding, he said, "Yes. Let's go."

The warmth that had blazed in her eyes less than a minute ago was replaced by a steely resolve that often indicated that Zara was ready for battle. She tugged on her suit jacket and smoothed the hair on her head. "I'll be there the entire time. Stick to the talking points, keep your responses simple."

Without another word, Zara turned on her heels and stalked off the field, muttering curses along the way about dirt, expensive shoes and cold Michigan weather.

Christian followed after her at a distance, taking in the scenery around him. The unusually warm March day was one for the record books. The Detroit skyline served as the backdrop, with the Renaissance Tower standing tall under clear, blue skies. Christian couldn't imagine living anywhere else.

His mother moved around a lot, having worked as a traveling nurse. Christian had lived in Chicago, Fort Lauderdale, Phoenix, Sacramento, and Tuscaloosa, Alabama all before he turned fifteen. When his mother took a job at St. Joseph Mercy Hospital in Ypsilanti, Michigan, he'd balked at the notion of leaving the warmer climate, another school, and his team at the time. But he'd fallen in love with the change of seasons, and later, with the state. It was destiny when he'd been drafted by the Detroit Jaguars, one of two professional baseball teams in the city. Although, he could technically go anywhere since he would no longer be bound by a contract, he planned to stay in the Detroit area.

Thinking of his mother, of the sacrifices she'd made to ensure he'd always had what he needed to thrive, put a damper in his mood. Because he missed her. She should be standing beside him when he made this announcement. She should be helping him run his mentoring program. She should be there. Period. The fact that she wasn't made his chest ache and his eyes burn with unshed tears. There would be time for emotion later, though. He couldn't give in to the sadness. Not now.

Christian brushed off his suit and straightened his cuffs as he stepped into the building. Turning, he spotted the bay of elevators ahead, leading to the offices and the player locker room. The press conference would take place there. *Zara's idea.*

Speaking of… *Where the hell is she?* He scanned the area. Few people milled around, maintenance workers readying the ballpark for opening day in a few weeks, cameramen hauling heavy equipment, team staff carrying out daily business. But no Zara.

Frowning, he checked the time. Maybe she went ahead to make sure everything was set up. He pushed the "up" button for the elevator. When the car arrived, he stepped on. Seconds later, he exited, stopping in his tracks at the sight of Meena standing there like she owned the place.

He drew in a slow, steady breath to calm his anger. They hadn't seen each other since the divorce proceedings, which was fine with him. His ex-wife had deliberately prolonged the process, instructing her attorneys to file motion after motion about everything, despite the existence of an ironclad prenuptial agreement. What should have taken sixty days had taken twelve months. During the settlement conference, security had to be called because Meena had threatened his attorney. Luckily for him, he'd hired one of the best attorneys in Southeast Michigan, a woman known as The Divorce Whisperer. When she was done with Meena and her attorney, he'd walked out a happy man.

"Christian?" Meena smiled, smoothing a hand over her long weave.

His gaze dropped to her attire. The sheer, skin tight dress she wore left little to the imagination, exposing swaths of her brown skin. They'd met at the now-closed Hard Rock Café Detroit during her lunch hour. He'd met Zara for lunch, and she'd come to the restaurant with her co-workers. Meena used to work for General Motors as a Financial Analyst. When they'd met five years ago, she was sweet, humble, and beautiful. And he'd fallen in love with her for all those reasons, and because she was nothing like the women who threw themselves at him after every game. But the woman standing in front of him now was nothing like the seemingly innocent woman to whom he'd proposed.

Over the two years, she'd transformed into another woman right before his eyes. Still gorgeous, but she'd developed an air of superiority that drove him insane. And her attitude? Nice-nasty and just plain rude. This Meena spent time staging her Instagram pics, shopping at exclusive shops and purchasing expensive brands. This Meena cared little about the people he was so passionate about.

"What are you doing here?" he asked.

"I needed to see you."

"For what? We don't have anything to talk about."

Meena straightened her shoulders. "I think we do." She stepped forward. "Christian, I hate how things ended with us. I didn't mean to hurt you."

Christian chose to remain silent. He'd been in this position before, faced with a remorseful Meena. Soon, the tears would fall. And when he rebuffed her yet again, the claws would come out.

"I just think we should clear the air. I've been thinking about you. I'm so sorry about your mom. I know how much she meant to you."

He folded his arms over his chest and narrowed his gaze on her. The passage of time hadn't dissipated the resentment he felt toward his ex. The heat of anger flushed through his body as she stood there, staring at him, waiting for him to make her feel better about her sorry attempt at "heartfelt" condolences. Because he knew better. He knew that Meena never cared for his mother. And he knew that because she'd admitted in court that she couldn't stand her.

The two had never really gotten along, but the already strained relationship between his mother and his ex-wife had been destroyed during the divorce trial. Rosalind Knight had never been one to hold her tongue, and Meena had gotten many an earful after the scandal broke.

She shifted on her feet. "When I heard she passed, I wanted to call you."

But you didn't.

"I tried to come to the funeral."

"Is there a point to this conversation? What do you want?" Christian could not stand there and listen to her pretend to care that his mother died. Meena wanted something from him and he would not spend another minute or even a dime over the court-ordered spousal support on her.

"I can't give my condolences to you? She was my mother—?"

"Don't," he warned.

"Christian, you—"

"This is a restricted area. How did you even get in here?"

She held up her All-Access pass, the one he'd given her last season when he'd made an effort to try to save their marriage. Before all hell broke loose.

Christian spotted a security guard to his left and walked over to him. "What's up, Ron?"

Ron Porter grinned. "Welcome back, Christian. The wife wanted me to tell you that she's sorry for your loss."

"Thanks. Tell Elaine I appreciate the flowers she sent. It meant a lot to me."

"I certainly will."

Leaning forward, Christian said, "See that woman over there?"

Ron looked over Christian's shoulder and his eyes widened. "You mean… that's your—"

Christian clasped the older man's shoulder. "Yes. That's her. Can you escort her out of the building? And make sure her access pass is destroyed because she is no longer Mrs. Knight."

"Sure, Christian. I'll get right on that."

Ron approached Meena and asked her to leave. As his ex-wife tried to cause a scene, screaming his name over and over again while threatening Ron with legal action if he touched her, Christian walked away.

Also by Elle Wright

Edge of Scandal Series

The Forbidden Man

His All Night

Her Kind of Man

All He Wants for Christmas

Once Upon a Bridesmaid Series

Beyond Forever

Jacksons of Ann Arbor

It's Always Been You

Wherever You Are

Because Of You

All For You

Wellspring Series

Touched By You

Enticed By You

Pleasured By You

DECADES: A Journey of African American Romance

Made To Hold You (The 80s)

Distinguished Gentlemen Series

The Closing Bid

Women of Park Manor

Her Little Secret

About the Author

There was never a time when Elle Wright wasn't about to start a book, wasn't already deep in a book—or had just finished one. She grew up believing in the importance of reading, and became a lover of all things romance when her mother gave her her first romance novel. She lives in Michigan.

Join the Elle Wright Reader Group!

Connect with Elle!
www.ellewright.com
info@ellewright.com

facebook.com/ellewrightauthor

twitter.com/lwrightauthor

instagram.com/lwrightauthor